THE INNOCENT

THE INNOCENT

Magdalen Nabb

CHIVERS
THORNDIKE

This Large Print book is published by BBC Audiobooks Ltd, Bath, England and by Thorndike Press®, Waterville, Maine, USA.

Published in 2006 in the U.K. by arrangement with Random House Group Ltd.

Published in 2006 in the U.S. by arrangement with Soho Press, Inc.

U.K. Hardcover ISBN 1–4056–1264 9 (Windsor Large Print)
U.K. Softcover ISBN 1–4056–1265 7 (Paragon Large Print)
U.S. Softcover ISBN 0–7862–8172–3 (Buckinghams)

The text of this Large Print edition is unabridged.
Other aspects of the book may vary from the original edition.

Set in 16 pt. New Times Roman.

Printed in Great Britain on acid-free paper.

British Library Cataloguing in Publication Data available

Library of Congress Cataloging-in-Publication Data

Nabb, Magdalen, 1947–
    The innocent / by Magdalen Nabb.
        p.   cm.
    "Thorndike Press large print Buckinghams."
    ISBN 0–7862–8172–3 (lg. print : sc : alk. paper)
    1. Guarnaccia, Marshal (Fictitious character)—Fiction.
2. Young women—Crimes against—Fiction. 3. Police—Italy—
Florence—Fiction. 4. Japanese—Italy—Fiction. 5. Florence
(Italy)—Fiction. 6. Rome (Italy)—Fiction. 7. Large type books.
I. Title.
PR6064.A18I565 2005b
823'.914—dc22   2005028016

CHAPTER ONE

It was one of those perfect May mornings, hot and fresh, with a sky that was paintbox blue. Even if he'd known what was going to happen, the marshal would have found it impossible to believe at that moment.

Lorenzini had tried to stop him on his way out. 'Don't you want a driver?'

'No, no. It's as quick to walk . . .'

And he had escaped from his Station, eager to be out. He could hardly explain to Lorenzini, his second in command and as down-to-earth a Tuscan as you could hope to meet. The thing was that, as soon as he'd opened the window in his little office and sniffed the sunshine, he'd known it was one of those mornings. The Florentines would be tuning up for the day with the maximum of noise and fuss. He emerged from the cool shadows of the stone archway into the dazzling light of Piazza Pitti, fishing for his sunglasses and, dead on eight o'clock, the conductor raised his baton. Hammers began ringing on scaffolding going up against the façade of the Pitti Palace, clanging away in time to a dozen tuneless church bells. Horns tooted as the first traffic jam of the day formed below the sloping forecourt around some roadworks. A pneumatic drill started up.

1

'Marshal Guarnaccia! Good morning!'

'Oh, Signora! Good-morning—how's your mother doing?'

'She should be out of hospital tomorrow. Mind you, we can't expect . . .'

What it was we couldn't expect was drowned out by the roaring drill and the marshal, with a vague, inaudible answer, pushed between the queuing cars and made for the bar on the other side of the piazza.

The bar was full of people having breakfast and the hissing espresso machine sent up wafts of fresh coffee. Three women, in summery outfits, stood blocking the counter, deep in discussion.

'Don't get me wrong, I've got nothing against her. She's a good woman, she's delightful, she's a saint, whatever you want! But she's a megalomaniac, that's all I'm saying!'

The marshal removed his sunglasses and stared at the speaker. She wore a lot of jewellery and looked as if she'd just been to the hairdresser, which she couldn't have at that hour, could she . . .? Over her head the barman indicated that he was already making the marshal's coffee.

He shifted away from the women's perfume in favour of hot jam and vanilla. It might have been the pleasure of the spring morning or it might have been those two bits of dry toast which were his breakfast these days, but he helped himself to a warm brioche and that was that.

'Of course, she means well.'

'Oh, of course!'

What a conversation! The marshal drank up his coffee and paid.

He couldn't get out of the bar because of an unruly snake of schoolchildren pushing and yelling, tumbling along the narrow pavement. A woman trying to get in lost her temper. 'They're allowed to run riot these days. It's disgraceful!'

Retreating behind his dark glasses, the marshal remained silent. If they couldn't run riot at that age, when could they? He was well aware that the sight of his uniform inspired people to blame him for just about everything, from undisciplined schoolchildren to the war in Iraq, not to mention that broken street light which, no doubt, would get mended now the elections were coming up. He joined the tail end of the school group moving towards via Guicciardini and the Ponte Vecchio. Their accents were northern, must be a school trip . . . People regarded him as one of the 'they' who 'ought to do something about it'. A large, pink-faced man was coming towards him, shifting on and off the kerb between pushing children and hooting cars, and trying to shake off a whining gypsy woman who was pulling at his clothes. The marshal paused and turned his black gaze on the gypsy who disappeared to attach herself and whine elsewhere. Well, it was true. They ought to do something, but what . . .? That fat schoolboy at the back whose friends were jumping on him and snatching at his backpack might have been his older son, Giovanni. Totò, younger, livelier and cleverer, ran rings round him. Giovanni, so like his father, had all his sympathy, Totò, his admiration.

He paused again. A pretty shop assistant emptied a bucket of soapy water on to the uneven flagstones in front of a leather shop and swept the suds into the road.

'Sorry . . .'

'No, no . . . Take your time.' He enjoyed the smell of the leather on the warm air. The girl smiled at him and went in with her bucket.

The children had pushed on, and were cutting a swath through the tourists on the bridge, while the marshal turned away from noise and sunshine into the gloom of an alley to his left.

He always chose this route for cutting through to via Maggio and the big antique shops these days. Traffic had been banned from going through, so he could walk in the middle and hear his own footsteps on the uneven paving, above the other sounds of hammers and rasps, radio music and snatches of conversation. Exhaust fumes had been replaced by the old familiar smells of glue and varnish, fresh sawdust and drains. And just

4

about at the halfway point between the two main streets, four of these alleys met in a tiny piazza. It was a higgledy-piggledy sort of shape and for most of its short life it hadn't even had a name. Recently, the residents had chosen one and put up a plaque they'd had made themselves. The reason for this was that the piazza had been created not by a Florentine architect but by bombs and landmines during the German retreat. *Luftwaffe* pilots, ordered to bomb the Ponte Vecchio, took very good care to miss it. The result of their excursions was the destruction of the buildings on either side of the bridge and the creation of this 'piazza' where a building at the crossroads had been mined to block the roads leading to the only surviving bridge over the Arno. It had quickly taken on the air of the real thing and filled up with restaurant tables and potted hedges. Fluttering from windows and brown shutters hung rainbow flags for peace, violet flags for the Fiorentina and fresh white flags for the medieval football tournament which would start in a few days.

'Morning, Marshal! How's it going?'

As usual, Lapo was on the doorstep of his little trattoria, grinning defiantly behind huge glasses across his four chequered tables at the grander twelve-table outfit a few metres away. His hands were stuffed under the bib of the apron down to his ankles such as his father and grandfather had worn before him. The sleek young things across the way wore trendy imitations of the same.

'Can't complain, Lapo. How about you?'

'Not so bad, not so bad. Have a coffee with me.'

'No, no . . . I've only just had one. I must get on.'

'So when are you going to come and eat with us? You're always saying you will. My Sandra's a good cook, you know.'

'I'm sure she is . . .' The good smell of herbs and garlic sizzling in olive oil, as she started her sauce for today's pasta, wafted from the open door.

'You'd be my guest, you know that.'

'It's not that . . .'

'No, well, I didn't suppose it was, not with the prices I charge. If you're thinking of eating across there you'll be wanting a mortgage.'

'I would never dream of going there, you can be sure of that.' The thing was that after years of being a grass widower before his wife joined him from Sicily, the last thing he wanted was to eat out anywhere. Going home to his own kitchen and finding family food and warmth was his idea of luxury.

As if reading his mind, Lapo insisted, 'Bring the wife and kids.'

'I will. That's a promise. Now, I'd better be on my way—how's it going with . . .' The marshal inclined his head to indicate the bigger restaurant. 'Are they still trying to buy you out?'

'Oh-ho, yes.' Lapo smiled broadly, flashing a row of shiny new teeth of which he was very proud. 'You can't imagine the amount of money they're offering, it's unbelievable! They've even told me to name my own price— there he is now.' The young owner appeared on his doorstep, black hair sleeked close to his head, black T-shirt, long green apron.

'Look at that suntan, eh, Marshal? He shut for two weeks in March to go skiing. The people I serve, work. I shut when they shut. What does he think I'd do with his money? Where would I go? This is not a job, it's my life, here with these people.' He waved a hand to include the packer who parcelled up bronze chandeliers and pieces of marble statuary for shipping abroad, the shoemaker, the furniture restorer and the printer. 'Of course, he's from Milan. You know the sort. They know the price of everything and the value of nothing. Well, he'll find me a tough nut to crack. I'm enjoying myself, to tell you the truth.' Lapo grinned and waved a cheery hand.

The younger man nodded and smiled, 'Good morning!'

Lapo shoved his hands back under the bib of his almost clean apron and muttered, 'I'll good-morning you, arsehole—you don't know what it means to have been born in this Quarter but you'll learn. What do you say, Marshal?'

7

Guarnaccia laid a big hand on the smaller man's shoulder and said, 'You stick to your guns. It'll be all right . . .' He hoped he sounded more convinced than he felt. As he walked on past the swishing of a printing press behind dusty frosted glass and the cool, fruity smell of ink, he wondered about Lapo, about all of these Florentines. He'd lived among them for so long, but every now and then he would get the feeling that they were from another planet. The young furniture restorer wasn't there. His shutter was down. He was often away up north, buying stuff. The shoemaker wasn't there either, though the door was open and the spotlight over his last was switched on. A young boy was working there, head bent low in concentration. Must be an apprentice. Yet weren't they all forever grumbling that it was impossible to get apprentices these days . . .? Captain Maestrangelo, his commanding officer, always smiled at the marshal's puzzlement, and it took a lot to get a smile out of him. Once he'd said:

—The world is made up of five elements: earth, air, fire, water, and the Florentines.

The marshal had stared at him, not knowing what to reply.

—Not my own, I'm quoting.

—Ah . . .

What was that supposed to mean? He should have asked Lapo about the shoemaker, a prickly, sharp-tongued man. His handmade shoes were famous all over the world, his quick temper a byword in the piazza. He'd had a heart attack last year and the doctor had ordered him to take it easy, not get so annoyed. Nobody, including the marshal, thought much of his chances.

He came out on via Maggio and started his round of visits to the important antique dealers, delivering this month's list of stolen pieces. Lorenzini had by this time given up saying: —We could send them e-mails. Probably he considered the marshal, who still prodded with two fingers at his manual typewriter, a hopeless case. It could be, though, that with experience he was beginning to understand that when a crime was committed it was too late to start getting to know your people.

The marshal, anyway, plodded on, going in and out of the big shops, breathing beeswax, mustiness and flowers, enjoying the dark-red polished floors, the inlaid woods, the antique brocades. If he worked for a lifetime and saved every penny he wouldn't be able to afford one piece from any of these shops but he could enjoy looking at everything. He'd never, as far as he could remember, seen a customer and he found it all strange except for Pino's shop on the corner of Piazza San Felice, his favourite and the only one where he lingered to talk. Pino wasn't like the others. His shop was just as big and grand, his pieces just as priceless but, though he wore a pale silk bow tie, it was peeping out above a white coat. He restored his treasures himself, together with his son, in a huge workshop below. He was a refined man, a knowledgeable man, that was obvious, but he was more like Lapo than like his fellow antique dealers and he had a greater passion for his work than for the money it earned him. No thief who knew his business would try to get anything past Pino, who accepted the marshal's list without comment and pushed it in a drawer without so much as a glance at it.

'Come downstairs a minute. I'm sorry about this . . . can you push your way through?'

Pino and his son were both thin and the dark corridor leading to the stairs down to the workshop was always lined with furniture and heavy picture frames. The marshal slid his sunglasses into his top pocket, breathed in and shuffled along sideways. He liked the room below, deep and shadowy with a high barred window looking on to the trunk of a palm tree in the spent light of a courtyard. A radio was playing quietly. Pino's son, in a pool of light, looked up from his work and pushed dark-rimmed glasses up to the bridge of his nose, smiling. There was no need of a pretext. Father and son both knew that the marshal enjoyed a look at their work when he had the time.

'How do you like these?' Pino asked: a set

of stools, low, square and heavy, the pale-green and gold decoration worn and faded over hundreds of years. 'Medici stools. I bought eleven of them when the Palazzo Ulderighi was sold off to that bank, but one's a bad one. Look.'

The marshal drew closer and peered at the one young Marco was working on. 'Woodworm . . .'

'Not woodworm. Somebody did a bit of cack-handed restoration work. Whatever happened to the original seat, this one's new. The woodworm holes are fake. Marco will probably do what we call a differentiated restoration where the added part is clearly differentiated, like this piece here, look . . .'

The marshal, watching and listening and understanding perhaps half of what was said, wondered what it must be like to have a father who had so much skill, such a treasury of knowledge to offer. He envied the young man. At once, envy was overtaken by guilt at the memory of his own father trying to teach him to prune the vines.

—Leave only three shoots no, no . . . You have to pick them carefully . . . one here on the left, this is a strong one in the middle and you pick the third one . . . that's it. Right, now snip it off clean. Now wrap the willow wand round and round and twist it . . . no, no . . . watch me.

So patient with such a clumsy son whose plump fingers never managed to twine the red

11

wand in a way that held. His father's fingers had black cracks in them but they also had knowledge. He'd offered what he had, knowing there was no future in it, wanting his children to get away.

'I ought to get on . . .' Had he interrupted Pino in mid-sentence? He did that sometimes, he knew. His wife had often said so.

—You don't listen to a word I say. You've got a conversation of your own going on in your head and you come out with some completely irrelevant remark and I'm supposed to know what you're talking about!

And the odd thing was that she always did. How did you explain that?

The morning mist coming off the river hadn't quite dissolved. The marshal rang Signora Verdi's doorbell, a top-floor flat round the corner in via Mazzetta, but no one answered. When he left the cold shadow of the high buildings in via Maggio to climb the exposed slope to Palazzo Pitti the sun was very hot. He had used up that first hour or so that ought to be spent on dull paperwork very pleasantly and was in good shape to deal with whatever his waiting room had in store for him. As it turned out, the tiled and windowless room offered up only two souls, one with a formal report to do with a small insurance claim, the other a small round woman of ninety-one with plump cheeks and big glasses.

'Signora Verdi! I told you I'd come and see

you. What are you thinking of, walking here and climbing these stairs?'

'I have to walk. If I give up now it'll be for ever—and what are your stairs compared with mine? Anyway, I came to thank you.' She reached for his arm and he helped her up.

'Come into my office. And don't be thanking me. If a few more people were as quick off the mark as you, there'd be less of that sort of thing going on. Come and sit down with me.'

'That sort of thing' was a yet another couple of cheap conmen in blue overalls carrying a clipboard and saying they were from the gas company. They claimed to be installing a new safety device at the back of all cookers, required by law, frightening old people with stories of explosions and going off with their signature and ten euros. Signora Verdi had told them she had no money in the house and asked them to come back the next day. They found two carabinieri waiting for them.

They had a little chat now, then Signora Verdi said, 'I'm going because that man in the waiting room was here before me. There's no banister on your stairs, though. Will that nice young carabiniere help me down?'

'Of course he will. I'll take you through. And whatever you say, you did a good job. I wish you worked for me.'

Once on her feet, she lifted her arms and gave him a little hug and, when he left her with carabiniere Di Nuccio, she said, 'My cooker's electric.'

The man with the insurance claim stood up.

'Come in, Franco, come in . . .'

Nobody else appeared after that, so the marshal found time for the paperwork he'd hoped to avoid and a quiet talk with a new man, not long out of NCO school, who wasn't getting on at all well lately. Nothing occurred yet to spoil his cheerful spring mood. When he stopped work and went back to his quarters, Teresa was in the kitchen, making spaghetti alla Norma, his favourite.

'I know you shouldn't have anything fried— but it was so lovely and sunny at the market this morning, I felt inspired—and you know the shepherd who comes on Wednesdays— well, it's not often he brings salted ricotta, so . . . Anyway, as long as you don't eat too much of it . . .'

He ate too much of it. It was wonderful. Of course, it's not the sort of thing you can digest without a glass of red.

A little sigh of contentment escaped him. Even when Giovanni and Totò started one of their interminable quarrels, he maintained his silent, beatific calm and let Teresa deal with it.

'Totò! That's enough!'

'Well, it's true! He's useless—and anyway, it's only because I want to be a software engineer. He doesn't even know what it means.'

'I do.'

'You don't. With a brain like yours you might as well be a carabiniere.'

'Totò!' Teresa shot her husband a quick glance and added under her breath, 'I said that's enough. Give me your plates.'

Giovanni gave up his plate and passed on his dad's. He looked crestfallen. The marshal, having only half followed the quarrel, wasn't sure why. He placed a consoling hand on his son's head but Giovanni cringed away from it.

Totò said, 'I don't want any meat.'

The marshal looked at his wife, who signed to him to ignore this.

Totò ate zucchini and bread. Giovanni ate everything and had cheered up by the time he was peeling his apple.

'I'll make the coffee.' The marshal exercised exclusive rights over the gleaming brass espresso machine. Teresa started the washing up and the boys went off to their room to start quarrelling over their computer games instead of doing their homework. 'D'you want it here or shall I take it through?'

'Take it through, I won't be a minute . . . the paper's out there. I haven't looked at it . . .'

He collected the newspaper that lay next to Teresa's handbag and the bowl of keys on the chest near the entrance. He shuffled with tray and paper into the cool, quiet sitting room and settled in a big leather armchair to enjoy that most precious hour or so before getting back into uniform. Teresa let her coffee get cold but she did join him briefly and told him a number of things without sitting down.

'So what do you think?'

'What? Oh . . . well, whatever you think best. If you want me to talk to the electrician—'

'Not about the new lights, about Totò? Anyway, tell me tonight, I haven't time to talk now.'

He was fairly confident that, whatever it was, she would tell him again. He never stopped being amazed by her, amazed that she should be there, looking after everything, telling him things and then, somehow, knowing what should be done. How did she know things the way she did, when he was so often baffled and full of doubts about the future? Letting this insoluble mystery go, he finished the article he was reading and then dressed with care for a visit to Captain Maestrangelo, across the river at headquarters in via Borgognissanti.

The captain was not smiling.

'I must just finish this call—no, make yourself comfortable . . .' He waved a hand at the black leather three piece suite and the marshal walked across and settled down, his hat squarely on one knee. A carabiniere came in and put a tray of coffee on the low table before him.

'Do you want the ashtray?'

'No, no . . .'

It was removed. One of the tall windows was

16

slightly open and a muslin curtain lifted on the faint afternoon breeze. The marshal waited, watching motes of dust revolve slowly in the shaft of sunlight that was warming the rug at his feet. After a while his gaze roved over the darkened oil paintings around the walls, overspill from a crowded museum. The captain was speaking into the receiver with such measured solemnity that anyone who didn't know him would imagine he must be talking to the President of the Republic. The marshal, who did know him, knew that he spoke like that to the humblest of his carabinieri. He liked him for it. He liked him for his quiet intelligence, too, and for his honesty and his seriousness. The only thing about the captain that irritated him—though he couldn't have said why—was when Teresa started going on about how good-looking he was.

—No, no . . . I'm not having that. No. He's a good man but . . . no.

—So elegant in his uniform and such beautiful hands.

—Hands?

'Don't get up.' One of the so-called beautiful hands, long and brown, grasped the marshal's own. The captain sat down and poured thick coffee into tiny gold-rimmed cups. 'So, were you able to make any sense of that business?'

'Oh, yes, no trouble. The signora was quite

17

right. You don't get an electricity bill like that if you've been in Provence and . . . where was it . . . Mexico . . . for the last seven months. No, no. I was pretty sure it was going to be the two young men on the opposite landing. I had to go round there twice because they must have spotted my uniform from their window that first time—I think I told you—so I got her to let me in herself at the street door this time and then she knocked at their flat and called to them. Once they'd opened up it was all over. I told her to switch the current off in her flat and they were plunged into darkness.'

'I imagined as much. How did they do it?'

'Nothing complicated. She'd had an air-conditioning unit put in and they got at that from their adjoining terrace and hooked up to it. She said she's not there that often so I suppose they felt entitled—you know how it is—rich foreigners putting up house prices and so on. American, is she?'

'French. She was Washington correspondent for a French newspaper for some years.'

'I see. She told me she's researching a book about the origins of opera now. That's a beautiful flat she's got and some very valuable antiques. I took the liberty of suggesting a more reliable burglar alarm.'

'You did right.'

'A charming woman.' A fine and elegant woman, too. Well, no doubt Teresa was right but he couldn't see it. There was no response

18

to this comment so he went on, 'I'm afraid she won't press charges. I couldn't convince her. Of course, they'll still be living next door to her and she's alone. You can understand it, really. I think they went to see her and talked her out of it, paid back some of the money. I can't make her change her mind and maybe she's right, after all.'

'It doesn't matter. You've solved the problem. Thank you. Is everything all right with you?'

'Never quieter.'

'And the man you were worried about . . . Esposito, wasn't it?'

'Esposito, yes. I don't know . . . I've had a talk with him but I'm just not sure. He's very distressed, very. Maybe there's something more than homesickness there and—besides, he seemed all right until just recently. I'll have to keep an eye on him. He's a good man, very serious. Very bright . . .'

They talked briefly about some building work to be done in the dormitories, held up interminably for lack of funds. Then they were interrupted by the colonel.

The marshal's driver brought the car to the foot of the stone staircase and they drove out through the dim cloister into the sunshine and bustle of via Borgognissanti. The marshal was cheerful and relaxed, well satisfied with a pleasant day. Only when they were driving under the archway at the Pitti Palace did something seem not quite right. An announcement was coming over the address system in four languages, warning visitors to the Boboli Gardens behind the palace that they should make for the nearest exit since the gardens were closing. The normal announcement that went out every day towards sunset. But it was only half past five and the sun was still high and warm in the blue spring sky.

CHAPTER TWO

'And where is this woman now?'

'No idea.' The gardener shrugged, on the defensive.

'But you took her name?'

'Took her name? As far as I knew, somebody was drowning. What would you have done? Started taking down her name and address and date of birth?'

'All right, all right. I'm not criticising, just asking.'

'And I'm telling you. I'm a gardener, not a policeman, for goodness' sake. I ran up here as fast as I could, which is what any normal person would have done. Not fast enough, though, right?' He cast a cold eye on the green remains of a face. 'Must have been in there a while. The fish did all right out of it, anyway. It's an ill wind . . .'

The marshal took a deep breath and advised himself to be patient.

'So that was all she said? That she thought somebody had fallen in the pool?'

'That's right—no, she did say which pool, for what it's worth. She said the one with the water hyacinths—that's this stuff and there's far too much of it, spreads like a weed but we've too much to do, so . . . There are a few pools and I'd never have thought to look up here, I mean, hardly anybody comes up here, why would they?'

'Two people did, apparently, if not three.'

'Three . . . ?'

That stopped him in his tracks. You had to bide your time with a Florentine who was acting cynical and aggressive to mask any emotional reaction. The marshal was something of an expert at biding his time.

'How do you mean, three . . . ?' His voice had become more subdued. 'You think somebody—you don't think she fell in . . .'

'How deep is the water?'

'About a metre, no more . . . maybe less.' He started to sink down on to the stone ledge.

'Don't. Don't sit down there. Stand away. Did you touch the body before I got here?'

'No, I didn't. I just looked. It took me a while to make out the . . .' He faltered at the word 'face', whch was hardly surprising. What there was, framed in a mass of bulbous green plants, was mostly bone with a few slimy shreds tangled up in pond weed and floating black hair. 'You can hardly see it—and you can tell by the plants I haven't moved it.'

'But you said "she". You said, "You don't think she fell in." How do you know it's a woman, or a girl?'

'I don't know . . . I suppose because of the handbag.'

'What handbag?'

'It was on the ledge.'

22

'And where is it now?'

'I'm feeling a bit—'

'Not there! Sit on that stone bench.'

'I'll be all right in a minute. I'm just a bit out of breath, that's all it is. What with running up and down this hill.'

'Sit there a minute and take some deep breaths. That's it. Now then, this handbag?'

'I took it with me when I went back down to my office to telephone you. I'll go and get it.'

'No.'

'It'll only take a minute. I think I'd better—'

'No. I don't want you touching it again. We'll collect it. And we'll have to fingerprint you, do you understand?'

But the man was clearly on the verge of being sick and the marshal took pity on him. 'Go and get yourself a glass of water and stay down near the Annalena entrance to give directions to our people and the van from the Medico-legal Institute.'

The gardener hurried off, his head down. Once his footsteps on the gravel had faded away there was no sound except for the chinking of blackbirds, hopping in and out of the low box hedging. It was true that nobody ever came up here. A stroll around Boboli was usually an extra, somewhere for tourists to relax after an exhausting visit to the big galleries in the Pitti Palace. Somewhere, too, for students from the language schools to eat a slice of pizza, toasting themselves on the broad ledges of the amphitheatre, watched by prowling cats. The mothers of Florence had their own well-worn routes. They pushed their prams idly back and forth as they chatted on stone benches under the plane trees of the long avenue or trundled their pushchairs on the gravel to the famous pools. They showed their children Poseidon stirring the waters, threatening the orderly lines of potted lemons with his trident, or the ferocious marble Oceano, ruling his island, and bright goldfish, bigger than the pointing toddlers, who appeared out of the green gloom, hoping for a crust of bread. Nobody climbed up here. A secret place for lovers to meet, maybe . . . sitting entwined on that smooth warm stone. A lovers' meeting gone wrong . . . or a discovery—

This thought was scattered as his memory, with a sudden jolt, threw up a sensation of panic and of his boots plunging into a raucous, flapping sea of hens and ducks . . .

Oh dear . . . even now he felt a hot flush of embarrassment at what would have happened if he'd been caught. Would his career in the army have ended before it began? Now he thought not, but at the time . . . Damn that priest!

It had been his first posting. Twenty-one years old, stuck in a village in the middle of nowhere. The woman was probably in her early thirties and he couldn't for the life of him

24

remember her name. Face like a madonna and a figure like Sophia Loren. She'd made no secret of the fact that her husband was shamefully neglectful of her needs and that he worked nights. And the church was right opposite. Of course, it was jealousy that made the priest call her husband like that and when she jumped up from the sofa at the sound of his motorbike there was no way out except by the kitchen window. He'd landed in the hen pen. Hens and ducks. Feathers everywhere and the row they kicked up . . . that was bad enough but at least he was dressed. If the husband had arrived ten minutes later . . . the risks we take when we're young . . .

'So,' he murmured to the ravaged skull in its green bed, 'what risk did you take?' It could have been drugs, of course, but he didn't think so. The gardens were closed at sunset, so this happened in daylight. An unlikely scenario. The marshal looked about him, wondering.

Water hyacinths, the gardener had said. Almost the entire surface of the pool was a carpet of pale round leaves and fat bulbous lumps. There was a small patch of dark-green water visible at the far side where a couple of ducks were eating themselves some space—that's what must have jolted his memory—but apart from that there wasn't a gap except for this small one. Spreads like a weed . . .

The marshal moved well away from the body—if there was a body—and got hold of a knot of the lumpy stuff. It bobbed on the water, attached to its neighbours but otherwise floating free on the surface.

'Hmph.' Well, that was all for the experts but as the marshal dried his hand on a white handkerchief, he couldn't help wondering, not so much that this death had happened but that it should ever have been discovered, that a face should ever have appeared from that solid green mass. He sat down on the warm stone bench and looked around him.

This sunken botanical garden was walled and with a high screen of laurel hedge beyond the wall. The pool was surrounded by a circle of potted palms and outside that began the low geometrical hedging of a formal garden. Very nicely clipped and so on, but really all this garden offered was seclusion. Whatever way you looked at it, it was difficult to imagine any reason to come here other than in search of privacy.

—Hardly anybody comes up here. Why would they?

Well, plenty of people were coming now. The marshal could hear the cars arriving. He stood up as the van came through the iron gates.

Two men got out and started to slide the metal coffin out from the back. They were stopped and made to move the vehicle by the photo-technician who had to take his long shots before coming in closer and saying to the marshal, 'Is it just a head or . . .'

'I don't know.'

'Better shift some of this stuff once I've done some close-ups.' But he was changing his lens. Shifting this stuff fell to two young carabinieri from Borgognissanti.

'What if it won't come up? We'll need the proper tools. Isn't there a gardener?'

'No, no . . .' the marshal said. 'We don't want to risk anybody else messing near the body. Just pick it up, it floats . . . that's it. Careful . . .'

But it was easy enough and soon a body was completely visible. Only the exposed face, neck and hands seemed to have been damaged, the rest, though swollen, was protected by clothing. The photo-technician moved in and the marshal, standing back with the two uniformed men, asked, 'Has the magistrate been informed?'

'The captain's seen to it. Should we go down and meet him at the entrance?'

'Yes, do. And if you don't see the gardener who sent you up here, knock on his door, the long low building on your left at the foot of the slope. Apparently he picked up a handbag . . .'

*   *   *

What with waiting for the magistrate and then the doctor, the sun was going down by the time the body had been removed and the marshal could sit undisturbed in his office, examining the handbag and its contents. The photo-technician had given it back to him after fingerprinting. It was his job to write a report and then send the bag in a wax-sealed box to the prosecutor's office. He intended to take his time. A woman's handbag was a treasure trove of information. As he sat and stared at the one in front of him in its polythene evidence sack, he remembered the first such bag to have played a role in his life, his mother's, a sacred object, never touched without express permission. He could remember one time when he'd been sent to fetch it, though he couldn't remember the occasion. A funeral, perhaps. The handbag, large, plain and black, only appeared on Sunday for Holy Mass or for weddings, funerals and christenings. Apart from market day, very much a shopping basket and purse outing, his mother never went anywhere. It must have been a funeral because the memory included the smell of beeswax candles. Probably his grandfather's death. There was no body in the image, but the absence of one was palpable.

—Bring me my handbag from the wardrobe.

There was no need to specify which wardrobe. There was only one. Standing in his parents' bedroom, he could hear his own heart thumping. The small low window was open but the outer shutters were closed and the air in the room was musty. A smell of mothballs

28

mingled with the beeswax. The high bed with its crocheted counterpane and the dark wardrobe seemed to him immense and the small lightbulb with its frill of glass illuminated little beyond itself. He could remember nothing except that moment but he assumed now that if the handbag was wanted, then it was to pay something to the priest who was sitting downstairs with the women, drinking a glass of zibibbo. The men were all standing outside. He could just hear their low voices and smell a faint whiff of fresh cigarette smoke drifting up. The money in the handbag was only for church expenses. Coins were given to him and his sister, Nunziata, for the collection at Mass. They had a particular smell, those coins, a mixture of mothballs from the wardrobe, the dab of lavender scent on their mother's handkerchief and sugared almonds, one of which they were given after Mass. They were always in the bag. They were favours saved from weddings and stayed in their little net bundles tied with a scrap of coloured ribbon. They in turn tasted of the mothballs, the coins and the dab of scent. Still, they were a treat and he was moved now by his mother's thoughtfulness in making something special out of so little. Had there been anything else in the bag? Apart from her big black rosary and small black missal . . . there was something that made him shudder . . . a bottle . . . not the scent, surely—smelling salts! In a frightening green bottle, a sharp burning stink that could choke you. It had once been used when his sister fainted in church. Afterwards, she had been put to bed, writhing in pain, and from then on he remembered that smell with fear. Nobody would tell him what was happening so he listened in on the whispering women in the kitchen as they prepared camomile tea with a teaspoon of honey in it.

'She's come on, bless her . . .

But what did it mean? Something from which he and his father were excluded, it seemed.

He removed the handbag from its sack. It was very different from the one his memory had conjured up, very soft leather, brown with the designer's initials printed all over it in gold, like printed cloth. Equally unlike his mother's, with its brief, unchanging inventory, this one was chock-a-block. Listing this lot was going to take some time. He tipped it all out and fished for a document in the pile of stuff. He found an identity card. Annamaria Gori, born in 1969 and resident in via Romana, not far, in fact, to judge by the number, from the Annalena entrance to the Boboli, about halfway between the Pitti Palace and the Porta Romana. Married name Bellini. He didn't recognise the face but these little photos they did for documents . . .

'So, what were you doing in that secret garden?' he murmured to the unsmiling face.

Mid-thirties . . . time enough to have tired of Mr Bellini. Not very attractive. Perhaps the rest of the bag's contents would tell him something. What a pile! The combined address book and diary, much scribbled on in pencil and various colours, contained nothing of interest. There was a dental appointment this morning which she certainly hadn't kept. Dead three to four days, the doctor had said. He went back a page or two but found nothing that looked like a meeting with someone in the Boboli. He put the diary to one side and pulled his old typewriter towards him to start the report with its long list.

Another address book, older and smaller, bank receipts, a fat wallet and purse with banknotes, change, a driver's licence and credit cards. Supermarket checkout slips, long ones, lots of them, dry-cleaner's receipt, a few visiting cards, a letter in a pink envelope, a leaflet from a candidate in the municipal elections, more receipts, restaurant, hairdresser, a very expensive fashion shop, two combs, one broken, three lipsticks, one of them used up, a large bunch of keys, a half-eaten bar of chocolate, an unopened bar of the same chocolate . . .

On and on went the list, telling of a life in which there was plenty of money, little sense and no order.

Four packets of paper handkerchiefs, two of them opened, five used and crumpled paper

31

handkerchiefs, three plastic ballpoint pens, none working, one gold fountain pen with empty cartridge, two brightly coloured felt tips, the pink one dried out and without its cap . . .

When the list was typed, the marshal pulled it off the typewriter and stretched, yawning. He was hungry.

Lorenzini opened the door. 'Have you a minute?'

'Mm . . . come in.'

'How's it going?'

'I don't know. There's a document in this bag with an address—just down the road—have you seen her about?'

Lorenzini looked at the identity card and shook his head. 'Mind you, these photos . . .'

'I know. I'll go round there now—you couldn't do the duty sheet for tomorrow, could you?'

'I already have. I didn't think you'd have time.'

Thank heaven for Lorenzini. He accepted the sheet and signed it. 'Anything else?'

'Well, I wanted a word about Nardi.'

'Oh, no . . .'

'It's not that I'm not happy to deal with it but they're used to you.'

'Well I've just about had enough of them. What's happened now?'

Nardi was a constant problem in his Quarter. What any woman saw in him a mystery, but two of them, his wife and his lover, had been fighting over him for years without any business resulting. Now, all of a sudden, the thing seemed to have flared up.

'You remember Monica came round to report the wife, saying she was threatening her?'

'Yes . . . ?'

'Well.'

'Well what?'

'She was right, that's what. Nardi's wife— what's her name—'

'Costanza.'

'Costanza, right. She marched up to Monica as she was coming out of the butcher's this morning and pasted her.'

'She what?'

'She's got a black eye and a cut lip and some scratches. She went to the hospital. It's official, and since she'd already reported the threat here, we'll have to take action.'

'Oh, for God's sake.'

'I know. Unless we can calm them both down.'

'But didn't Monica defend herself? She's a bigger woman. They say that's why Nardi . . . I mean . . .'

'Yes, well, she got in a few good scratches. Long nails.'

'Long red nails, yes. Oh dear . . . If you do think you can cope, I really ought to deal with this Boboli case. The thing would be to try and find out why this dust-up happened. They've

33

been going along comfortably for years.'

'I'll do my best. It beats me, though. I mean, it doesn't happen these days, does it?'

'What do you mean, it doesn't happen? It is happening.'

'Yes but . . .'

But Nardi, a retired railway employee who still performed Sinatra numbers at the railway workers' social club, was over seventy. His thin, cross wife, Costanza, and his big-breasted 'bit of fluff', Monica, were both in their late sixties. Passions ran higher in their generation, apparently.

'Do your best to stop her going through with it. You know it'll be a waste of time. She'll change her mind long before it comes to court.'

'I suppose so . . .'

'You don't seem convinced. It's not the first time, though it has been a few years.'

'Yes. It's just that she says she's trying to get on that TV programme—you know—the one where they have a judge and they settle family quarrels and condominium disputes and stuff like that.'

'Good. Let them sort it out and give us a rest.' The marshal was feeling around in one of his desk drawers where he kept a lighter, a stick of wax and his seal. 'I'd better get this stuff ready to go first thing in the morning. How's Esposito?'

'Just the same. The men say he barely

speaks and that he spends all his spare time shut up in his room.'

'Does he? Well, he soon won't be able to do that. With any luck the builders will be starting work on the new bathrooms any day now. He'll be battling with dust and mess, shut in his room or not.'

'So will we because the builders are going to be trailing through the waiting room with their wheelbarrows. It'll be a nightmare. Anyway, the lads don't think he's homesick. They say he's been like this since he worked on that suicide case with you. The trouble is, being an NCO, he can't confide in any of them. Oh, and Di Nuccio—who's Neapolitan too, after all— says he's probably in love.'

'Oh, no. What is the matter with everybody, all of a sudden?' Even the captain and that Frenchwoman . . .

'It's spring. Let me pack that for you if you're going round to this woman's house. It's supper time.'

The marshal made some telephone calls, the last one to his wife.

'I don't know . . . not long, I hope. Start without me . . . You have? No . . . no. Lorenzini did say it was late but I didn't realise . . .'

He closed up his office.

It was a little girl who came to the door of the first-floor flat in via Romana. She was perhaps six or seven, very slight with long

35

brown silky hair.

'Come back here!' shouted a woman's voice from somewhere down a long corridor. 'Nicoletta! Let your dad go to the door.'

The child flashed a knowing smile at the marshal and shot off along the red-tiled corridor on a plastic scooter. The marshal waited. He had announced his visit but not explained it. He had no idea whether he was here to comfort or to investigate. A man appeared from a room on the left carrying a forkful of spaghetti.

'Come in. What's it about? I'm sorry but we're having supper. Nicoletta!' He caught the scooting child on her return journey and ran along beside her, trying to insert the fork in her mouth. 'Just one. Come on, just one.' The child turned her face away from the fork and scooted off. Returning, she stopped dead and, with her triumphant gaze fixed on the marshal, allowed the fork to pass her lips before scooting off again.

'Roberto! Who is it?'

'Somebody from the carabinieri! I told you they rang! Come this way.'

A pleasant and surprisingly large room with french windows on to a terrace behind and a lot of green beyond. Turning to look at him from the dining table were a stolid, big-eyed boy and the woman of the identity card. She was very heavily, if lopsidedly, made up and very much alive.

'Do sit down . . . Marshal,' the husband said. He didn't say where and left the marshal to decide for himself while he wound more spaghetti on to a fork from the bowl in front of an empty chair.

'You're going to have to stop giving her chocolate.'

'It's the only thing she'll eat. What do you want me to do? Let her starve?' The woman poured herself half a glass of red and looked at the marshal. 'What's the matter? Has something happened?'

'Nicoletta! Come back here!'

'I'm not hungry!'

The marshal glanced over his shoulder and saw the scooter flash past the doorway pursued by the forkful of food. At the table, the boy shovelled and sucked at his spaghetti, oblivious.

Perplexed though he was, the marshal was grateful for the distraction of all this rushing about since it gave him time to rearrange his ideas. The woman had asked him for an explanation of his presence but seemed no more interested in whether he answered than in whether her little girl ate anything. He decided to say, 'I think you lost your handbag today.'

'Oh, thank goodness, I knew I must have left it at the supermarket—that's the second time I've done that—you can't imagine what a day I've had without it. I had to pick the keys

37

up from the daily woman—my mother has keys but she'd already gone to pick Nicoletta up from school and take her to dancing class . . .'

The little girl shot in through the door, scooted round the table and out again, always with that little triumphant smile on her face which, though she never looked at him, was directed at the marshal.

The father was winding another forkful from her bowl. 'Have you made that appointment with the pediatrician?'

'I think my mother might have, I'll ask her tomorrow afternoon. We're going shopping.'

The little boy spoke up: 'She's supposed to be taking me to football practice tomorrow afternoon.'

'Roberto! Can you take Marco to football practice tomorrow?'

Whether he answered yes or no, the marshal didn't notice. The woman's hair was much crimped and brightly coloured though very untidy, but what amazed him was her make-up. It was orangey brown and thickly plastered on, and each eyelid had a bright-green slash which might as well have been aimed at her by the child dashing past on the scooter. It gave her a wild look, though she was clearly unruffled by life and her smug, smiling expression was a practised version of her daughter's.

'Marco, go and bring a glass for the

marshal.'

The boy slid down from his chair obediently.

'No, no, Signora . . .'

'Shh!' When the boy had left the room, she leaned forward and whispered, 'Don't say anything to Roberto about the handbag. He's already annoyed about the pediatrician and I'm not telling him that my mother's already taken her. He said she could be running a very slight temperature all the time and that's why she has no appetite. He said he wants to do blood tests, can you imagine? I've no intention of letting him. I can't bear the thought of them sticking a needle in her, wouldn't you feel the same?'

'I—'

The little boy returned with a glass and sat down. He took a piece of bread and mopped up every last bit of sauce from his pasta dish, then handed over the clean plate underneath for some of the big frittata that was in the centre of the table next to the salad bowl. The marshal, watching him, thought that at least this fluffy-headed woman cooked. It was late. The frittata looked good and he was hungry.

'Are you sure you won't have a drop . . . ?'

'No, thank you.'

'Mum! It's onions again. I don't like the onion one.' He didn't stop eating, though.

'Well, I can't help that.'

'Why can't you tell Miranda I don't like

onions?'

'I have told her.'

'Well, tell her again.'

'Do you want some more?'

While she was serving him another large slice, the little girl came skipping in and started dancing round the table with a bar of chocolate in her hand, followed by her worn-out father who sat down in front of a bowl of pasta which must, by now, have been quite cold. The marshal, knowing he was going to have to get this woman into his office, away from the husband, if he wanted to get any sense out of her, stood up.

'I'm sorry to have had to disturb you.'

The husband was getting to his feet.

'No, no . . . I'm sure the signora will show me out as she's finished her meal . . .'

He looked grateful. Through a mouthful of cold spaghetti he said to his wife, 'What was it about, then, did you witness a road accident or something?'

'Your wife could be a witness to an accident, yes . . . nothing to worry about. Excuse me.'

At the door, he turned his gaze on the woman in what he hoped was a threatening manner. 'Signora, you didn't leave your handbag at the supermarket. It was found by the pool in the upper botanical garden in Boboli.'

Until then, he hadn't suspected her of anything more than woolly-headed selfishness and chronic laziness, but now her eyes were suddenly glittering and her face under the plastered make up flushed dark red. 'If I didn't leave it at the supermarket, somebody stole it. At the checkout when I was packing my stuff. They must have done. I saw a bunch of people there who looked like Albanians to me. If you found the bag in the Boboli they'll have dumped it there when they'd taken what they wanted. That's what they do, isn't it? Were my keys still in it? Because if they're not I'll have to be in when Miranda comes every morning until my mother gets some new ones made for me—she'll have to do it because I'm not telling Roberto. Did you notice if they were there?'

'Yes, Signora, they are.'

'Well, you could have brought the bag with you, couldn't you? Saved me all this trouble.' It was fortunate that she was saying all this in an aggressive undertone so the husband wouldn't hear, otherwise she would have raised her voice to him. How did her husband stand her? The marshal considered himself a patient man but Roberto was a saint.

'Signora, I'd like you to come to my office in the carabinieri station at Palazzo Pitti to sign for and collect your handbag. Not tomorrow because I shall have to get the magistrate's permission to release it.' He said this slowly and quietly, more calm and expressionless even than usual. Anyone who knew him would have been alarmed by this.

'What a pain! And, in any case, it won't be before eleven because I'm going to the hairdresser's the day after tomorrow and she's redoing my streaks, I want them blonder. It costs a fortune to have them done and it takes so long it's exhausting, so at least they should show up—'

'And when we're in my office, Signora, you will tell me the exact circumstances in which you discovered what you thought to be a drowned person and why you left after mentioning the fact to a gardener.'

'You mean it wasn't a drowned person? Was it a dog or something? It was something disgusting, anyway—oh, well, never mind.' Had he been of a more manageable size he had no doubt she would have pushed him bodily out of the door, which she slammed behind him. What an awful woman!

*　　　*　　　*

'So what does she do all day then?' The light was on in the warm kitchen. Teresa cut him another slice of bread and sat down to keep him company. She was fascinated. 'If she has a cleaner every day who cooks as well, and her mother's running around—or driving around—all the time for her . . . does she go out to work?'

'I hadn't thought . . . no, I can't imagine anybody employing her—besides, what about the hairdresser and the afternoons in the Boboli? No, no . . .'

'What gets me is that she didn't care that you knew she was lying—you know, when you said about the gardener and all that.'

'Mm . . . well, I doubt if she cares what anybody thinks. Even so, there was something she wanted to hide . . .'

That alarmed glitter in her eyes, the dark flush under the slapdash make-up.

'Maybe she meets a man in the garden. You said yourself you couldn't imagine any other reason for going there.'

'There are plenty of things happening in the world that I can't imagine. I can't imagine how that woman's husband can stick her for a start. If anybody's in need of a bit of light relief, it's him.'

'Well, then. Maybe she found out. Of course, not many men have time to be up to no good in the park in the afternoons. What does he do?'

'I don't know. I'll have to ask.' It crossed his mind that women would do a better job at finding out other people's business and understanding what was going on. Odd, really, that most detectives were men who couldn't find their own socks.

'Is there a bit more bread?'

'You've had your allowance. I'll cut you half a slice.'

Of course, he wasn't a detective himself. If

43

this turned out to be a complicated case, the captain would have to send a real investigator, a plain-clothes man, from Borgognissanti headquarters. Not that he ever did. The captain was a good man, a serious man, but he'd got it into his head that Guarnaccia could deal with anything so he couldn't expect any help from that quarter. It was true about women, though. If Teresa had been telling him this story she would have known every detail about the family, including what was wrong with the little girl and what should be done about it—and she'd have understood right away what the woman was hiding. But, of course, women, being more sensitive . . . but that meant, surely, they wouldn't want to have anything to do with murder . . .

They were very often the victims, that was true . . . they had to do with murderers.

That dreadful green eyeshadow woman hadn't turned a hair, though, when she saw the drowned face and dumped the problem on the gardener and he'd almost fainted.

So, you couldn't really say . . . he let this mystery go, took a sip of wine and finished the last scrap of his frittata. It was so good.

'Do you want any more?'

'A bit. I just fancied a frittata tonight and the onion one's my favourite.'

She looked puzzled. 'I know that.'

'And that reminds me: what's this business about Totò? I'm not having him running about not eating.'

'Running about not . . .? That woman's really got on your nerves, hasn't she? Anyway, listen: Totò's decided he's a vegetarian. Now, it'll probably wear off but don't, for goodness' sake, say anything to him!'

'Me . . .?'

'The more attention gets drawn to it, the more he'll stick to it out of pride. You know what he's like.'

'Hmph.' Out of pride? How could anybody resist a Florentine beefsteak, especially with chips, out of pride? He'd have said it couldn't be done. Or roast rabbit . . . with fresh herbs and olives and a splash of dry wine the way Teresa always did it . . .

'Were you saving some of this for tomorrow?'

'No. Finish it. Another drop? The electrician's left his estimate . . .'

CHAPTER THREE

Esposito was driving. It had seemed like a good idea to the marshal, to get him out and about, do him good. It had seemed like an even better idea to Lorenzini who'd had about enough of his long face around the place and enough of Nardi and his women, too. The marshal had given in on that one. So their first call took them to the heart of the San Frediano quarter. It was mid-morning. Women stood talking outside the baker's and there was a big queue in the butcher's where Costanza had attacked Monica. At another corner of the tiny crossroads stood what had once been Franco's bar where everybody used to hang about and gossip, have elevenses and watch the match in a fug of cigarette smoke on Wednesday nights. Franco's bar had been a godsend long ago when the marshal had been investigating the death of poor mad Clementina. Franco knew everything about everybody and he'd kept the peace and settled disputes like a tribal chief of the Quarter. If he'd been here now there would have been no need for the marshal's visit. But Franco had died and now the dusty bottles and football rosettes, the pinball machines and Formica chairs, had given way to tourists and pink tablecloths, 'No Smoking' and microwaved pasta followed by salads for a light lunch. Across the road from the bar, Nardi was leaning on his elbows at the first-floor window, his face turned up to the sun, his shirtsleeves rolled up, smoking. He saw them at the street door in the shadows below and withdrew to open up. What he wanted was sympathy. What he got was a lecture. The marshal didn't consider himself to be an unreasonable man, but in his opinion a man who had his work cut out coping with one woman had better not take on two. Admittedly, he'd managed all right for donkey's years—with a bit of help from the marshal—but perhaps the truth was that the women had somehow managed up to now. Well, he certainly had his tail between his legs this morning. The three of them stood in the brown ceramic-tiled entrance hall. Nardi was wearing those flat felt slippers that clean the floor as you shuffle.

'Listen, Marshal, you've got to talk to her.'

'To your wife?'

'No! No! To Monica! She's threatening to—'

'I know what she's threatening, Nardi, but if you want to stop this thing now, you're going to have to get Costanza to apologise, at least.'

'I can't do that—d'you want to come and sit down? She's out shopping.'

A cloud of smoke was drifting inside the open door of the sitting room that gave on to the street. 'No, no . . .'

Nardi kept shooting unhappy glances at

Esposito. Probably, he was embarrassed by the presence of so young a man. With an inward sigh, the marshal sent him back down to the car.

'Thanks. I didn't like . . . come and sit down a minute.'

'No, I can't. I have to get to the Medico-legal Institute. Just tell me what it is that's started all this fuss. You've not been neglecting your wife, have you? You know what I'm talking about.'

'What, me? No, no, no. My wife's never had to go elsewhere for it.'

'So what's happened, all of a sudden?'

'She wants to leave me, that's what's happened!'

'Monica?'

'No! Costanza!'

'Why do I have to talk to Monica, then?'

'So she'll convince Costanza to stay with me!'

'So she'll— Listen, Nardi, this is bound to blow over. It has before. And besides, where's Costanza going to go?'

'She's not going anywhere!'

'Well, then!'

'I'm the one who has to go. She's leaving me but this was her mother's house. She expects me to get out. It's me who's supposed to find somewhere to go. Are you with me now?'

'I . . . and Monica . . . ?'

'She lives with her mother, you know that.

48

She's a nice woman, I'm not saying anything against her, but she's nearly ninety and what I'm saying is that—just for example—if I want to trail round the house in my underwear when it's hot, that's what I do. I can't live like a guest in somebody else's house. D'you follow me?'

'Well, yes, but if she's nearly ninety, after all . . .'

'She's in better shape than you or me. Probably outlive me. So will you talk to her?'

'What, the mother?'

'Monica!'

The marshal had been exhausted by the time he got away. Nardi never seemed to bother putting his dental plate in. He only had four teeth of his own and, what with age and nicotine, they weren't very nice teeth, not very nice at all. It made you wonder . . .

As they drove along, he decided that he would definitely try to get Lorenzini on to it and if they weren't used to him they'd better get used to him. Four teeth . . . Young Esposito beside him was a good-looking lad, no question about that. Tall, dark and handsome—perfect teeth, too—Teresa seemed to be very taken with him and his beautiful smile. Wondering if the lad was in a fit state to drive, the marshal gave his attention a nudge. 'Just look at this traffic. It's going to take us an hour at this rate.'

The traffic was just as bad today as it was every other day and it always did take an hour.

49

Yet despite all the exhaust fumes, the car was filled with perfume from the lime trees in blossom along all the avenues so the journey wasn't unpleasant. It was just that Esposito's morose silence was much more irritating than Nardi's diatribe. The marshal comforted himself with the thought of a meeting with Professor Forli at which both Esposito and himself would be kept on their toes, paying attention and trying to answer questions which the professor would answer himself before they could open their mouths. The Medico-legal Institute was a department of the University of Florence. Professor Forli was a teacher, a gifted one, and every year he gave a series of lectures on forensic pathology to the students in the carabinieri NCO school, disconcerting them by his unusual method of delivery. The system was his own invention and he was very proud of its efficiency. He recorded the lectures beforehand and played the tape to the class, striding up and down the room with his hands clasped behind his back, listening to himself, until he couldn't resist intervening. After that, he would talk over himself, saying the same thing as the tape, word for word, until he became irritated by the competition and snapped his recorded self off.

One carabiniere student had drawn a cartoon of him in which the balloon coming out of his mouth and the one coming out of the tape recorder were both saying: 'Now, most of the flies involved in the early stages of decomposition have maggots of three stages, the first, second and third instars . . .' Photocopies were passed around the school and, of course, a copy eventually fell into the professor's hands. When the marshal and Esposito arrived and were sent down the broad marble corridor to go into Forli's office and wait there, the cartoon, pinned on a notice board behind his desk, was the first thing they saw. It was rather a good cartoon. The gaunt professor's chin was jutting out, his big hands clasped tightly behind his back. Esposito looked at it and then at the marshal. 'He wasn't at all annoyed.'

The marshal who had known Forli for many years said, 'Why should he be? Did you survive his autopsy?'

'I was all right. It was only the smell I was worried about. Anything really bad makes me sick but it wasn't that terrible . . . They all say, though, that he . . .'

'That he sees to it that it's always lasagne on the canteen menu that day.'

'Is it true?'

'Of course it's not true! As if professors have anything to do with canteen menus. That story's been going the rounds for years.'

'Yes. I've never eaten lasagne since, though.'

There. The professor had worked his magic before he even arrived in the room. Esposito hadn't put two sentences together like that for days.

'Good-morning, good-morning, good-morning!'

'I'm afraid we're disturbing you . . .'

'Not at all. Pleasure to see you, Marshal. Your drowned woman, right? I haven't dissected the internal organs yet, apart from her lungs to establish whether she drowned, and he's asked for a tox report, too. What's the panic? You people always say it's the first forty-eight hours that count. They're long gone in this case. Got a lead, have you?'

'No, nothing like that.' He didn't try to explain why he was there. He knew all the facts would be in the autopsy report. It wasn't the facts that he wanted. What he wanted was a glimpse of the things Forli knew but didn't write. Some people had an instinct for understanding the living. Forli had one for understanding the dead. He talked to them during his autopsies. They didn't lie, he said.

'She did drown, then? I wondered, with there being so little water . . .'

The professor had turned his eagle eye on Esposito. 'You're not long out of school. How much water would I need to kill the marshal here?'

'One drop, sir.'

'If it went where?'

'Up the nostril with enough force to hit the olefactory nerve, sir.'

'Don't call me sir. And what would happen

to the marshal's heart?'

'Could be paralysed, ss—'

'I thought I remembered you. Esposito.'

'Yes.' The young man flushed a little under his brown skin. His eyes were alight. The marshal had almost forgotten but that's how he used to look.

'Well, don't try and kill the marshal with a water pistol, Esposito. I doubt, knowing him, that his sympathetic nervous system is of the sort to amplify small disturbances. Your woman drowned all right, Marshal—pond life in the lungs—but she had a bit of help: she took a blow to the back of the head—can't tell you much about it because of decomposition but something sharp. Nicked her skull. She could well have been unconscious when she drowned.'

'We didn't find any possible weapon nearby. And it would have been something to hand, wouldn't it? I mean, you wouldn't choose to murder somebody in a public park. Of course, it's a very big park and we're still looking, but unless we're lucky enough to find something with blood or hair on it . . .'

'As likely as Esposito's killing you with his water pistol. I'd look in the pool, if I were you. She only had one shoe on. People sit on those stone ledges around the pools. So: one shoe. Esposito?'

'Somebody could have picked her feet up and tipped her backwards into the water . . .'

'And?'

'And she hit her head.'

'Drain the pool, Marshal.'

'Yes. We have to anyway. We found no bag, no documents. A young woman would have had a bag of some sort, I think . . .'

'Drain the pool. Pity about her hands. They could have told me a lot. As it is I can only tell you young—late twenties, I'd say, seems healthy, non-smoker—so: what else is she telling us?'

The professor began striding up and down the room, chin jutting, hands clasped behind his back, oblivious of his audience. Some ten minutes or so went by and he hadn't stopped for breath . . .

'Now, that was an interesting case for many reasons. What could we see? That he hyperventilated leading to pulmonary oedema and hypoxia whereas the other one I mentioned, our example number three . . .'

Only the tape recorder was missing. Both the marshal and Esposito were unable to resist a quick glance at the cartoon and then at each other. That was a mistake. Esposito was soon suffocating with nervous laughter which eventually exploded, despite the hand clapped over his face. The professor stopped midstream. 'Are you all right?'

'Yes! It's an allergy. Pollen from the limes. I sneeze all the time in May. Excuse me.' He covered his face with a paper handkerchief.

The marshal fixed the young man with huge solemn eyes. The professor was soon going full steam again and forgot they were there. When they tried to leave, he offered to let them look at the drowned woman's lungs through the microscope. The marshal had to drag Esposito away.

When they were back in the car the marshal, more than a little impressed by Esposito's performance, said, 'You seem to have learned a lot.'

'Yes, it's an interesting subject, not like law or, even worse, the military stuff we had to do. Besides, he's a good teacher.'

'Yes. But you must have been a very good student. He remembered your name. He told me once he's been known to hesitate when he has to sign his own name if he's really concentrating on a problem.'

Esposito didn't answer. He had retreated into gloomy silence again and the marshal reined in the desire to try to get to the bottom of his problem and scold him into cheerfulness. What was the use when he'd said all he could think of to say just the other day? He'd do better to be thinking about the problem of the builders who hadn't turned up this morning. Their story was something to do with the building permit. When it was only internal stuff you were supposed to be able to start three weeks after depositing the plans. Like as if . . . the Palazzo Pitti was the Palazzo

Pitti and it was inevitable that the state would send an inspector . . . but when? He'd better let Captain Maestrangelo know. The captain paid attention to the details of life, all the more so if they affected the well-being of his carabinieri. It wasn't that they couldn't manage with just the two shower stalls, it was the immersion heater that was the problem. They needed constant hot water. As things were, when two lads had taken a quick shower there was no more hot water for half an hour. Still, it seemed unlikely that Esposito would cheer up even if he could have a long hot shower instead of a quick tepid one.

They drove back through the city centre. In the cathedral square, droves of tourists blocked their way. Esposito waited glumly as tour guides with raised umbrellas ploughed through the crowds or paused in a pool of shadow to point up at the white and blue marble bell tower sparkling in the sunshine above. In via Guicciardini, tourists were spilling off the narrow pavements, many of them biting into big slices of pizza held in brown paper. The whole street smelled of freshly baked dough and peppers and tomatoes.

'Lunchtime,' commented the marshal happily.

They turned left up the slope to the palace.

Esposito parked the car in silence. Before going to eat, the marshal called the head

56

gardener and made arrangements for the pool to be drained.

*   *   *

The water had to be syphoned off and it took hours. It was hot. In a matter of days the order would go out to change into summer uniform. In the meantime, the carabinieri sweated and the gardeners worked first in shirtsleeves, then in vests. They were going to have to leave enough water for the fish but that wasn't a problem. Once it was low enough, they would spot at once any object which had only been there a few days. Everything else was covered in slimy green plant life. The marshal stood, as he always did, well out of the way of those who were working, in the shade. The gardeners' conversation was centred on the water they were syphoning, which was now running away down a lightly wooded slope beyond the garden.

'What a stink. Not the sort of job you want to be doing in the sun. Stagnant water's a bad enough smell on a winter's day.'

'I just wish we'd had this water to play with last summer. In all the years I've been here—and that's plenty—we'd never lost a tree before then. I wouldn't have thought it possible, I wouldn't.'

'They say this summer it'll be back to normal.'

57

'Let's hope so.'

A few bunches of water hyacinths, their soft roots dripping like long black hair, were tied into plastic bags half filled with green water to be taken to other pools. Beppe, the oldest gardener, small and round and brown as a nut, knew the marshal well. He offered him a bagful.

'It makes a lovely pale-blue flower, like an iris. Take some. You've got a bit of garden. Make a nice little water feature for yourself.'

'No, no . . . I wouldn't have a clue . . . no.'

'Only need to say the word, you know that.' They trimmed the laurel hedges and raked the gravel around the carabinieri station in the normal way of things but it had never gone much further than that. The old gardener didn't hurry away.

'Bad business . . .'

'Yes.'

'They say it must have been a murder . . .'

'Do they?'

'Giovanni thinks so. He says a child might drown in it but not an adult. That's what he says.'

'Mm.'

'Of course, there's drugs . . . or drink, maybe. You get these young foreigners who drink too much. Away from home . . . We get a lot of them in here. Eating pizza, leaving litter . . .'

'Mm.'

'I suppose you shouldn't be talking about it like this.'

'No.'

'No offence meant—it's just that in our job we like to have something to talk about while we're working. It passes the time. Not another word, then. Right.'

But he didn't go away. The marshal, understanding what was wanted, talked to him, asking about his wife's operation, his eldest daughter's new house, his newly married grandchild who was still living at home, unable to find a flat so if the marshal knew of anything . . . The marshal knew of something. He was well aware that this would translate into all sorts of confidential information and dark hints about murder when the old gardener rejoined his mates. Before he did, he looked up at the marshal and whispered, 'We've got a bet on. I reckon that, however she got in there—Giovanni thinks drugs, the others say she was pushed in—she probably slipped. *Spirogyra*. Very slippery stuff. Cracked her head on a piece of the statue.'

'But there are no—'

'Marshal!' They'd found something. The marshal came forward into the light, stepping over the plastic hoses with care.

A carabiniere was holding up a shoulder bag.

'Open it.'

'I can give you some rubber gloves if you

want.'

'No. Just open it.'

They spread the contents on a plastic sheet. It was bad news. The bag contained nothing that could identify the drowned woman. No document, no wallet, no scrap of paper. When every zip compartment had been opened there was still nothing. There were some keys which were no help at all without an address. There was one of those pouches for loose change that the banks gave out free along with a little plastic bag of coins when the euro was introduced. There was a comb in a leather case and a ballpoint pen.

The marshal took out the notebook he always kept in his top pocket and gave it to the carabiniere. 'See if the pen works.'

It did. 'Is that a help?' the carabiniere asked, surprised.

'Yes.' A functioning pen, a clean, unbroken comb in its case, coins in their pouch. He was willing to bet that if her entrance ticket to the gardens wasn't in her missing wallet or one of her pockets it had been dropped into a waste bin, not on the ground. There were no sodden paper handkerchiefs here, no half-eaten—blast that woman! She hadn't appeared to claim her bag.

'Something wrong, Marshal?'

'Yes! No. No . . . Call the oldest gardener over here, the one with the straw hat, putting his shirt on. Can you see him? Get him here.'

60

The gardener approached, buttoning the check shirt over a round belly, his face alight with interest and self-importance. 'Have you found a clue?'

'What statue?'

'Eh?'

'You said you thought she'd cracked her head on a piece of the statue.'

'Well, I was just saying that, you know . . .' He faltered, his face red. 'I was just saying that. It's not that I . . .'

The marshal fixed his black gaze on the small round man. 'What statue?'

'The little lad with the fish, like the one at the Palazzo Vecchio. There was a bit of a fountain here once but it wasn't much of a thing. Nice enough, you know, but it was only a poor copy so when it got smashed up nobody bothered. The bits are still in there—they kept this garden padlocked for a long while after that because of vandals—'

'Padlocked? When was it reopened?' The marshal was feeling for his notebook. Just one verified fact in this case would be something.

'Oh, it's a while, now . . .'

'When?'

'Well, my eldest was still at home, that I do remember. Might have been seventy-one—no, I tell a lie, it was seventy-two.'

The marshal put his notebook away.

'Have I said something I shouldn't?'

'No, no . . .'

'You had me worried for a minute, there. I mean, I was just saying that about the statue. It's not that I—you don't think that I really know something—'

'What are you talking about? I just wanted to know about the statue, that's all, because you're very probably right.'

'I am? Well, I thought—nobody can tell what you're thinking behind those glasses. You want to take them off when you're talking to people.'

'Sorry. You've been a help.'

Beppe went off to rejoin his mates, no doubt bursting to tell them he'd been right, the marshal said so.

The marshal stood looking down at the low green water and now he did take his glasses off. The flickering orange of a spotted goldfish drew his attention. It was swimming round and round something, the tip of which appeared just above the surface. He dried his sun-sensitive eyes, put his dark glasses back on and called to his carabinieri. They netted a marble fish and put it into an evidence sack. It had been the tail fin which was sticking up, impossible to tell yet whether the soft black strands wrapped round it belonged to the water hyacinths or the victim.

Professor Forli would be as pleased with himself as Beppe. The marshal mentally took his hat off to them both.

Later, listening to all this, Captain

Maestrangelo gave all the credit to the marshal. 'Now, is there anything you need? I know Lorenzini can be relied on when you have to be out but I hope you have enough men because—'

'Oh, yes. Thank you. Yes. What I need is a list of persons recently reported missing. A young woman like that must have parents, a husband or boyfriend, a job. Somebody would miss her.'

'I'll see to that for you—was she wearing a wedding ring?'

'I don't know. There was no flesh left on her hands, so . . . If she was and it came off in the water we'll find it. We're sifting through everything near where the body was found. And, of course we're still looking for the other shoe around the whole area.'

'Odd sort of thing to carry away. Not a likely weapon, I take it?'

'No, no. Quite a broad heel, rubber, too. No.'

They were in the captain's office and it was nearly eight o'clock in the evening. The scent of limes coming through the open window was almost overpowering. As was often the case in the afternoons, the captain was in civvies.

'I'll get the list of missing persons to you first thing in the morning, and we'll put something in the newspaper and on the regional TV news.'

A carabiniere came in and interrupted

63

them. The captain stood up. 'If there's anything else, wait for me.'

'I will, if that's all right. I wanted a word about Esposito.'

Waiting alone in the quiet, spacious office, the marshal thought about Esposito. He'd just announced that he wanted to leave the army. The army could ill afford to lose him. His story was that he felt he should find work nearer home, in Naples, because he was an only son and his widowed mother was ill. The marshal had asked him what sort of work, what sort of career opportunities he thought he'd have in Naples. The young man had only looked at him with dazed eyes full of pain.

Remembering Lorenzini's mention of that suicide case—a young man who'd left a wife and child—which had, it was true been very distressing, he suggested, 'Are you worrying about your mother? Do you need to get home for a few days?'

'It would help, yes.' He had looked so grateful.

Well, it could have been the suicide case but if it was, he was going to have to toughen up. And if, on the other hand, Di Nuccio was right and a woman was the problem, well . . . the thing was to rescue his career now and hope he'd get over it later. Most people did. There were men who didn't, not completely, and they ended up marrying somebody cosy and pleasant who didn't provoke such strong

64

feelings, maybe somebody a bit more like their mothers. There were those, of course, who never got over it, full stop. The sort that never got over anything. Couldn't fancy the risk of provoking another catastrophe, threw themselves into work, lived like monks. That was no way to go on. A man should live like a man. The marshal remembered taking Teresa round when she and the boys first moved up here from Siracusa. They'd visited the Certosa Monastery, a museum now, and been shown round by a monk whose habit and breath suggested he had lunched a little bit too well. He had shown them the tiny cells with their bloodthirsty frescoes and hatches just big enough to admit a plate of food or a book. Then he'd leaned forward, breathing wine fumes, and told them in a confidential tone, 'That sort of life . . . well, it's not suited to us Italians.'

Nor was it. The marshal gazed about him now, remembering that this barracks was once a monastery. There was still a bit of a fresco over the captain's oak door . . . Thinking it over, he decided he'd be wise not to dwell on the personal aspect of Esposito's problem with the captain but to concentrate on not letting the army lose a good man, serious, intelligent, with a bright career in front of him.

It was the right thing to do. The captain decided that Esposito should be sent home for a couple of weeks on compassionate grounds, given his mother's illness, and that, on his return, the captain would call him in for a pep talk about his career.

'Thank you. I think that'll do the trick and, if it doesn't, well, you can only do your best . . .' The marshal got up to leave.

'I'll walk down with you. I have an appointment on the other side of the river.'

They went down the stone staircase and stood a moment in the cloister, waiting for the marshal's car to be extricated. The voices of carabinieri echoed loudly round the rear courtyard as three other cars had to be shifted.

'Keep more to your left and watch that pillar!'

'You might have to move the jeep!'

Their engines roared, unnaturally loud in the confined space.

The captain's mind seemed to be running partly on the worry of restoring the centuries-old flagstones of this, their only entrance and the chaos it would cause, and partly on Esposito's future in the army.

'In my father's day young officers of good family served their country with us and didn't even take their pay.'

'Times have changed a bit since then.'

The marshal's car pulled up.

'You might drop me on the other side of the river, Guarnaccia.'

Bats dived under the bridge and swooped in large circles in a red sky, feeding on mosquitoes. The perfume of the limes hung too heavy, now, on the still air. The captain got out on the left bank and the marshal watched him disappear in the evening shadows of a narrow street—the one he had recently visited himself—without comment.

The carabiniere driving asked, 'Back to Pitti, Marshal?'

'Yes.'

'Good. I'm starving . . .'

CHAPTER FOUR

The marshal probably grumbled, though not always aloud, as much as anyone else. There was a perpetual voice of conscience, though, that warned him to count his blessings. Given the job he did, there was always ample scope for things to get worse. So he sat in his office on the morning of the first of June and did a bit of mental book balancing. Twenty-nine degrees was too hot for June, everyone said so. His men were having to cover their beds and belongings with cellophane every day and wash with a series of buckets. Builders were trundling wheelbarrows through the waiting room, taking out rubble and bringing in sand and cement. A thick veil of cement dust lay everywhere. It penetrated the marshal's office and every file in every drawer felt chalky. Esposito had entrained for Naples and he was one man short. Neither an article in the local paper nor a brief mention on the regional news had produced any useful information about his drowned woman. There was no one on the missing persons list that was the right age.

And to cap it all, after two hours of drudgery among his dusty files, he now had to face that woman. What was her name again . . . ? He fished out the appropriate report and blew on it with a sigh. Annamaria Gori. All right. Things could be worse: twenty-nine degrees was hot for the beginning of June but the nights were still cool so you could sleep. It was miserable for the men without their shower but it would have been a lot worse in July or August. What's more, if the place weren't full of dust and chaos, he'd be annoyed because the builders hadn't started work. Given that they had started, they'd soon be finished. Then, Esposito was at least off his hands for a while and he'd done what he could. Might be an idea to give him a ring next week.

Teresa had been very concerned:

—I do hope you don't lose him. There's something about him, I don't know quite how to describe it. I mean, all your boys are very kind and well-mannered to me but Esposito . . . he always looks as though he really means it, d'you know what I mean? Of course, he's a beautiful-looking boy but it's not just that. When you talk to him his face kind of lights up . . .

I don't want to keep him in the army because of his smile, for heaven's sake!

'Marshal? Somebody to see you.'

'All right. Show her in.' Keep remembering that things could be worse. At least the blasted woman had turned up at last—and, you never knew, he might get something useful out of her.

He didn't. On the other hand he did find

69

out what she was doing in that garden. He should have noticed at the time that she identified the pool by the plant growing there.

'I wish you'd told me before. I'm trying to find out how a woman died. It's a serious matter.'

'But it's nothing to do with me, though, is it?'

The two slashes of eyeshadow were bright blue today. It was difficult not to stare at them. Was she just slapdash or . . .

'Tell me something, Signora. Do you ever wear glasses?'

'No. I ought to but I don't like myself in them.'

'I see. And are you short-sighted or long-sighted?'

'I can't remember. One or the other. Roberto says when I renew my driving licence and they test my eyes I'd better get contact lenses, otherwise, if they stop me and I'm not wearing glasses, I'll get in trouble.'

'He's quite right.'

'Still, now I know you, I can come to you if I get in trouble, can't I? I wouldn't mind contact lenses but I couldn't fancy putting them in and besides, you have to keep washing them and I'd be dropping them or losing them all the time. Wouldn't you? Then he'd be annoyed.'

'What does your husband do, Signora?'

'He's an optician. So you see, he'd be moaning at me every time I lost them.'

'And you don't fancy wearing glasses. So you thought what you saw in the water might be a dog.'

'I touched it, can you imagine? It was something disgusting, I could see that, and it stank, so I told that gardener he should see to it. I mean, I could have caught something!'

'Sign here, Signora, will you?'

'What does it say? Roberto says I should never sign anything without reading it.'

'It says you've received your handbag and checked its contents.'

She signed without reading it. As he showed her out, he suggested, 'Next time, Signora, buy your plants from a nursery.'

'Well, if I had, I bet you'd never have found that woman so you ought to thank me. They're not flowering yet but Roberto's already moaning on about the stone sink they're in being too heavy for the balcony. He's expecting it to hit the woman underneath on the head any minute, can you imagine? She's a pain in the neck anyway, always moaning if Miranda puts the washing out. When did a few drops of water do anybody any harm? Still, if she keeps on being a nuisance, I can call you now, can't I, after I've helped you?'

Once she'd gone, the marshal sat himself down at his desk with a determined frown on his face. What he determined was that Annamaria Gori was to become Lorenzini's exclusive client. Along with Nardi. They were all Tuscans and should understand each other.

He picked up the missing persons list which one of Maestrangelo's men had helpfully asterisked to indicate people reported missing in Tuscany. As he had expected, there was nobody the right age. Children got lost, or were abducted, unhappy teenagers ran away, often in pairs, to reappear after three days or so when the money ran out. Disappointed older men, their personalities and their dreams eroded over the years, walked away in amazing numbers and never came back. Very few women in that age group. Young women in their mid-twenties left their husbands, changed their jobs. They didn't need to escape, they could just go . . . except illegal immigrants. A very few young immigrant women escaped from the sex trade. Not nearly enough. If only she had a face . . . and hands, her hands could have told Forli so much. If only Forli would—

The phone rang. It was Forli.

'I was just thinking about you!'

'Thinking, "Why doesn't he get those internal organs done?"'

'Well . . .'

'Sorry. You know how it is. That drugs shoot-out, a suicide and the post-operative . . . Anyway, I've done yours now and I'll get the written report to the magistrate tomorrow; but there was something I thought you'd want to know quickly. She was pregnant—ten weeks. Could be the beginnings of a motive so I'm looking at the DNA of the foetus. I've started to track the woman's dental work but you know how slow and difficult that is unless we're very lucky Another thing: I cleaned off the skull because it doesn't look Caucasian to me. Mongoloid, I'd say. Now, it's possible, these days, to determine race, which might help you. Unfortunately, I can't do that here but I have a colleague in London who'd do it for me. Amazing chap. I'll get a sample to him right away.'

But . . . the bureaucracy—'

'No, no, no! No bureaucracy. A little bit of research between friends. You don't know this man. They once turned up some fragments of a skull on a building site and he spent every spare minute he had on those fragments until he'd rebuilt the skull, modelled the face and given the woman the right sort of hairstyle for the period when, according to his calculations, she died. Put a photo in the papers and on TV. Solved a thirty-year-old murder case. A case like this one he could see to over his breakfast with the crossword. He has a passion for crosswords. I'll give him a ring tonight—no, tomorrow night. I've got nothing on tomorrow night and, believe me, when he starts talking about his cases, you'd better have nothing else on. He'd talk the hind leg off a donkey. Good man, though. Very good man. I rang him once on a case, I don't know if you remember it . . .'

Some fifteen minutes later, the marshal

hung up and rubbed at his ear. It felt hot. His spirits, however, were much refreshed and when Lorenzini came in with some evidence bags he found the marshal in good humour.

'What have you got for me?'

'Her clothes. Dried out and tested in the labs. Not good news, I'm afraid, as regards hard evidence, after so long in the water, but all bought in Florence. Good quality and well-known labels. Nothing from the marble fish— same thing, the water. They're sending it to Forli anyway, to check it against the shape of the wound. That's it. Any luck with the missing persons list?'

'Nothing. Is there anybody in the waiting room?'

'An elderly couple. English. A stolen—or more probably lost—bag. Their passports were in it so the consulate sent them over here to report it.'

'English . . .'

'I'll deal with it.'

'Thanks. I want a bit of peace to look through this stuff.'

He caught a glimpse, as Lorenzini went out, of a passing wheelbarrow pushed by a wiry little man with a hat pushed to the back of his head and a cigarette dangling from his mouth. The English couple stood on a piece of corrugated cardboard, looking perplexed. The door closed.

He had asked the builders four or five times

74

not to smoke in the waiting room. Each time they said, 'Don't you worry, Marshal. We shan't be wanting to use your waiting room. We only light up when we go out to the truck. All right?' And forty times a day they left their trails of smoke. The youngest one sometimes remembered and stopped to grind his cigarette butt into the tiled floor.

Things could be worse. He'd seen some boxes of tiles. They were on the last leg . . .

The marshal sat down and removed each piece of the drowned woman's clothing from its bag and laid everything out on his desk.

Underwear: plain white cotton, bought in the department store in Piazza della Repubblica. Dark-blue linen sweater, label of a big, expensive fashion shop near the cathedral, elasticised blue jeans, the label cut out, plain white shirt, label cut out but a small white V embroidered on a pocket. Unmistakably Valentino. A very simple necklace of coral beads. A belt, pale, natural leather, narrowish, rather a nice buckle, and a maker's name impressed on it. No cutting that out.

The marshal stared at the name, trying to decide whether to be pleased or not. There was nothing surprising about it. The woman had been found in this Quarter and there were only three possibilities when it came to hand-made leatherwork of that quality. He was pleased to have a solid fact to go on but he'd have been even more pleased had it been one of the other two. Peruzzi, the crossest shoemaker in town. The only hope was to catch him in a good mood though, of course, he probably had no reason to remember this customer. Unless she was a regular. Unfortunately, the single shoe didn't carry his name. It looked like a handstitched shoe but you would expect the maker's name to be written on the inside and there was nothing. Besides, it was a funny sort of shoe. It was a very low bootee with a small heel and a pointed toe, laced up the front. The sort of thing he remembered his grandmother wearing, though hers were black and this one was pale natural leather like the belt. What was strange, though, was that one part of the shoe seemed to be different from the rest. The rest was all perfectly smooth and pale, but the left side was a little darker and had a different texture. Of course, it had been in the water but he couldn't imagine that would account for it. Well, Peruzzi could help if he had a mind to and, if not, the marshal would certainly be spending the rest of his day away from the dust and noise. He collected up the clothes and called for a car.

*   *   *

'I'm sorry about this. Be careful of . . .' The piercing whine of three electric drills drowned

76

the rest of the shop manager's warning and the marshal followed her through a cloud of dust, stepping over a tangle of cables, to a tiny room at the rear. There was corrugated cardboard on the floor and filing cabinets and stacks of boxes were swathed in polythene. 'It's meant to be finished before the menswear fair starts but I'm beginning to doubt it. You can't imagine what it's like trying to work in the middle of all this mess and the noise . . . Let me close this door so we can hear ourselves think.' She looked around and started shifting polythene sheets. 'I don't think you'd better sit down, unless . . .'

'Don't worry, I'll stand. I just want you to look at this sweater. You might have seen on the news or in the paper that we're trying to identify a woman who was found drowned.'

'I'm sorry. I never read the crime page.'

'It doesn't matter. If you'd just look at this—it is your label—genuine, I mean? There are so many fakes about.'

'No, that's ours. Besides, I recognise the sweater. It's last year's, though.'

'And I suppose you sold hundreds of them.'

'Hundreds, no. A linen knit as fine as this is very expensive. Over five hundred euros. Even so, I have five sales girls here and, with so many customers being tourists, we really don't know them all.'

'Of course not. Would your last year's accounts show anything? If there weren't all that many sold, if she paid, let's say, with a credit card?'

'I suppose it's possible . . .' She was a very nice woman, about the marshal's own age, her grey-blonde hair simply dressed, her clothes quiet, and you could see she would have liked to help. 'It's just that, in all this mess and with the winter collection to organise for when the fair starts and the summer sales right after that, I don't know how we'll find the time. I really don't.' She opened her hands to indicate the chaos around her, frowning. She was wearing hardly any make-up and he could see brownish rings beneath her eyes.

'What if I sent you one of my men and you—'

'No! That's the last thing I need! I'm sorry, but if you could just wait until the workmen have gone. It should only be a day or two.'

How could he not sympathise? He gave her his card and took one of hers. Picking his way out through dust and noise, he hoped, for her sake as much as his own, that it really would be a matter of days. She would help him if she could, he felt. Besides, he had learned one thing: over five hundred euros for an everyday sweater to wear with jeans meant that the drowned young lady had money. He got into his car and gave directions to the carabiniere driver, bracing himself for an interview with the angry shoemaker.

'It's closed to traffic,' the driver reminded

78

him. 'Shall I go through anyway?'

'Yes.' He was trying to remember any occasion on which the shoemaker had been calm and cheerful. All he did remember was the time a pyromaniac had set fire to his car. Still, he needn't have worried. The apprentice was alone in the workshop, standing at a workbench, his back to the door.

'Good-morning.'

The young man was cutting out a piece of leather on a slab of marble, using a sort of scalpel, freehand. He finished his stroke and put the knife down carefully before turning with a smile.

'Go to shop, please.' He pointed. 'Borgo San Jacopo.' He wasn't Peruzzi. What's more, he was obviously Japanese and there was going to be a communication problem. On the other hand, he was certainly calm and cheerful.

'Is Peruzzi in the shop?'

'No Peruzzi. Today hospital.'

'I see. I need to talk to him. Will he be here tomorrow?'

'Yes. Today hospital.'

'And you're his apprentice? How long have you worked here? A year? A month? How long?'

'Yes. Ten months.'

Was that long enough to make it worth asking him anything about the shoe? He'd know more about it than the marshal did, at the very least. He opened the bag and held the

79

shoe out. 'Can you tell me anything about this shoe? Anything at all?'

The smile vanished.

'You recognise it? Was it made here? Is it Peruzzi's? A copy?' He was breaking every rule. Suggesting, talking instead of listening and watching. It was because of the language problem. But words are not everything. The young man was worried. He took a step backwards away from the proffered shoe, glanced behind him and then stood still. The marshal sat down on a polished wooden bench and remained silent. If you leave enough silent space, people rush to fill it out of fear or embarrassment. He placed his hat and sunglasses squarely on his knees and waited. He didn't stare at the apprentice but let his eyes rove around the workshop. There was a show window, mostly hidden from view by a linen curtain on a brass rail. He could see into one corner of it and out at the little square. Some people, particularly regular customers for whom Peruzzi had made shoes for years, came here rather than go to the smart shop on Borgo San Jacopo. There, casual customers and tourists were dealt with by a patient woman, well away from any danger of encountering Peruzzi whose gimlet eye and raucous Florentine voice would have scattered the customers like a fox scattering chickens. The young man still didn't utter a word. And yet there was no real tension in the air, just silence. Like the silence of an empty church. Why should that be? The strong smell was of new leather so it wasn't that. The light perhaps . . . a narrow beam of sunlight beside the linen curtain and, elsewhere, the gloom pierced only by a lamp on the workbench. The one over the last was switched off. Not the light, then . . . this bench. The long, broad bench he was sitting on might well have come from a church. Its smoothness owed as much to hundreds of years of use as to polish. The armrests were carved.

Not a word from the apprentice. It had never happened before and the marshal didn't know what to do. Should he repeat himself to fill the space? Can you tell me anything about this shoe? Wouldn't that be ridiculous? He decided to look at the young man, try to judge his attitude.

His attitude was one of polite submission. He stood quite still, his thinness accentuated by a long canvas apron that reached his ankles, his hands folded in front of him, his head very slightly bowed and his gaze lowered. Baffled, the marshal looked away and saw, through the window, Lapo passing by behind his bit of hedge with two plates held high.

He stood up. 'I'll come back tomorrow and talk to Peruzzi about this.' He slid the shoe back into the evidence bag.

The young man smiled and bowed his head just a little more. 'Thank you very much.

Goodbye.'

The marshal replaced his hat and glasses and went out. His driver wound the window down.

'No, no . . . take the car back. I want a word with a few of the people here and then I'll walk. It's only a couple of minutes. Do me a favour and let my wife know I'll be late.'

The car moved off slowly through the narrow space filled with pedestrians.

'Lapo!'

'Oh, Marshal! Come and sit down. Come on! You can't say no today. Sandra's made a polio alla cacciatore that's out of this world. Sit here where I can talk to you.'

'You're busy . . .'

'Don't worry—Sonia! Come and say hello to the marshal!'

Lapo's daughter, Sonia, was very plump and looked older than her sixteen years but she was pretty, her skin clear and rosy. She shook his hand.

'Take over here, Sonia. Let me have a chat with the marshal—and bring Santini some more bread with his chicken.'

When she'd gone in, he said, 'There's no "table number two" and "table number four" here. I know my customers and they all have their regular places and their regular times.' This with a black look in the direction of his rival over the hedge. 'What do you think of my daughter, eh? Is she a treasure or isn't she?

There aren't many like her these days. We're lucky.'

'That's true.'

'They all want to go to university, whether they've the brains for it or not. And none of them want to work hard or dirty their hands. And where's it going to end? Have a glass of red with me.'

'No, no . . . on an empty stomach . . .'

'You're right. I eat before we open.' Lapo blocked Sonia as she passed carrying a plate of chicken in a glistening tomato sauce and a basket of bread. 'Leave this bread for the marshal so he can have a drop of wine with me while he's thinking what to eat and get some more for Santini.' He waved the basket at the young restorer at the far table. 'Sorry! She'll bring yours right away.'

Santini raised his glass in salute and grinned.

The marshal nodded. 'That's a talented lad.'

'You're right there,' Lapo agreed. 'But he'll never make any money. He spends weeks restoring those old kitchen cupboards with the painted flowers on them that he buys up north and then sells them for half what they're worth. He always says he just enjoys doing his work and if he keeps things hanging around with a high price on them he'll have no room for new stuff to buy and work on. Good health, Marshal.'

Sunlight splashed through their glasses to

make two wine-coloured spots dance on the white paper covering the table. The bread was crusty and fresh, and that chicken smelled so good . . .

'What were you doing at Peruzzi's place? He's at the hospital today for an ECG.'

'So I heard. I went in to ask him about a shoe we found. It belongs to somebody we're trying to identify—I'll tell you about that in a minute, if you haven't already seen it in the paper.'

'Not me. Politics only. And I can tell you that these elections—'

'Yes. I know how involved you are but I need to know about Peruzzi.' And the last thing he needed was for Lapo to start sounding off about politics. 'There's an apprentice there . . .'

'Issino? He's a good lad. A treasure. Bit funny till you get used to his ways—you know how the Japanese are.'

'Careful.'

'Eh?'

'I've never yet had a Japanese tourist in my office who's lost his camera or had his pocket picked. There was a stabbing once that involved a Japanese journalist and a band of gypsy children. Stabbed him in the leg near the station but we only found out by accident because he got his train to the airport and left for Japan, bandaged up with his own first aid kit. He fainted at the airport and one of our

84

men got the story out of him so it got around, but there was no stopping him getting on that plane.'

'I can't say I blame him.'

'No. But what I mean is I never come across them because they seem to be so sensible and careful. This lad—what did you say his name was?'

'Issino—well, that's what we call him because his real name's Issaye, or something like that, and it's a bit difficult for us Italians. I'm not saying it right now, I don't think.'

'Issino . . . he seemed—I don't know. He wasn't keen to talk.'

'Issino? No! Santini! The marshal's asking about our Issino, says he's not keen to talk.'

Santini put down the bread he was dipping into his sauce and laughed. 'Get him to tell you the one about St Peter and the prostitute, but you'll have to finish it yourself.'

'Sonia! Chicken for the marshal and a green salad. Green salad all right? Green salad and another quarter of red! Issino's learning Italian and he wants to be able to tell jokes. He reckons that's the test. You should see him. He struggles and struggles through the whole thing with everybody prompting him with the verbs and then, when he gets to the punchline the only line he knows by heart—he cracks up laughing and can't get it out.'

'He eats here, then?' The marshal glanced over the low hedge at the workshop but nothing was visible beyond the displayed shoes and the partially drawn linen curtain behind.

'Once a week. But the other days he comes over for a coffee and a chat, and what he calls his Italian lesson. He hasn't a bean. I think he eats something at his bench the other days.'

'Peruzzi doen't pay him much, then?'

'Pay him? He doesn't pay him. He's teaching him. That's how it works these days, Marshal. Foreigners come here to learn from our artisans and pay them for the privilege. Take on an Italian kid of fifteen who has to be taught everything and produces nothing for years and you're into paying a wage plus huge contributions. Nobody can afford it. It's a policy that's all wrong and if the Left can't get itself together and realise the damage—'

'This apprentice,' interrupted the marshal firmly, accepting his chicken from Sonia and reaching for the bread. 'He must have money or how could he afford to be here at all? He must have rent to pay and if he doesn't eat much, he still eats.'

'That's not the way it is. Listen. He used to work in a shoe factory, somewhere near Tokyo, don't ask me to pronounce the name. He told us they have a raffle every year for the workers and the prize is a trip to Europe. You must have seen Japanese people, poor-looking, coming out of Gucci loaded with bags? They're factory workers shopping for their friends who didn't win the trip. Stuff here costs a tenth of what it costs in Tokyo. Anyway, that's how Issino first came here and he decided that he wanted to come back so he saved every penny and here he is. He'll stick it out, too, not like Akiko. We were all surprised that Akiko left but Peruzzi was beside himself. Best apprentice he's ever had, walked out, just like that. You probably heard about it—no? Well, anyway, whichever way you look at it, it's all skill that's going out of the country. Our grandchildren will have to go to Japan to find a pair of Florentine shoes and to China for a bottle of Chianti—no, no, you can't sit with us. The marshal and I are having a talk.'

The printer and the packer had arrived together.

'What's for dinner?'

'Pollo alla cacciatore.'

They settled down at Santini's table and shouted for Sonia.

'Excuse me a minute.' Lapo got up reluctantly. The four outside tables were occupied now and people were piling inside as all the workshops closed. 'I'll have to let Sonia go back inside. Let these other two places go, but keep mine. I'll be back so we can talk a bit more. I always like talking to you. Eat up, now.'

The marshal thought that Lapo liked talking to anybody and wondered at the patience of his hard-working wife and daughter. But the day was hot and sunny, the

87

company lively and the chicken very tasty indeed. So he ate, thinking of the quiet Japanese boy in his long apron, trying to square what he'd seen of him with Lapo's description. He replayed their encounter in his head as he chewed. The failure to be provoked by silence had thrown him but, apart from that which, after all, could have been the respectful good manners of a different culture, what was there? A worried look at the odd shoe, a glance behind him. He had no money. He ate over there at his workbench almost every day. Peruzzi wasn't paying him.

He flagged down Lapo who was carrying away dirty plates.

'This apprentice . . . strictly between ourselves and what you tell me I won't hear—he's living there behind the workshop, isn't he?'

Lapo shrugged and raised his eyebrows without a word.

'All right. Come back for a minute when you can. I need to ask you something else.'

While he waited, he mopped up every last trace of sauce with his bread. He really should bring Teresa and the boys. Giovanni's birthday was coming up . . .

'Right you are, Marshal. What can I tell you? Oh—you'll not cause any trouble for Issino?'

'For living there? No, no . . . It would be Peruzzi who got in trouble, if anything.'

88

'And you know he can't afford to get upset, what with—'

'I know. Don't worry about that side of it. What I want to know is about the other apprentice, the one who's gone. Does Issino have a girlfriend, that you know of?'

'Issino? No. He used to hang out with Akiko—they were good friends—but I never saw him with a girlfriend.'

'And this Akiko. Did he have a girlfriend?'

'Akiko? Don't you know Akiko? Did you never get to see her? Prettiest Japanese girl I've ever seen, like a doll. Bright as a button, though, and tough. I'm surprised you were never introduced. Must have been jealous, wanted to keep her to himself, eh?' He winked. 'I'd have done the same myself. Peruzzi always said—'

The marshal stopped him. 'I'm going to wait until you've finished here and then we need to talk seriously. Don't say anything to anyone else.'

'What's the matter? I haven't offended you, have I? Just my little joke, about him being jealous. I meant nothing by it. There's something wrong, isn't there? I hope you're not going to tell me something's happened to Akiko.'

'I don't know, yet.'

'I'll be back.' Lapo took the marshal's plate and went about his business. The marshal took out his phone and called Forli. He was pretty sure he would be eating on the terrace of the big restaurant on the hill behind the hospital city with his colleagues and had no qualms whatever about interrupting him.

'What? Ah! you've found out something, then. Yes, certainly Mongoloid would include Japanese. I'll get something from London in a day or two—and given the state of the body, you'll have a problem if somebody has to try and identify her so we'll need those results whether you've got a name or not. Keep me informed!'

He waited for Lapo. The clattering of plates and the rowdy talk faded comfortably into the background as he examined the fragments of a picture in his head. Two young people from the other side of the world, so determined to learn a skill. A thin young man in a long canvas apron, a young woman as pretty as a doll. And tough. He didn't understand but he would find out. She might be a Japanese girl from the other side of the world but she had died here on his territory, in his quarter. He would find out.

CHAPTER FIVE

Walking back, he made detours through a number of shadowy back alleys, so narrow that the sun had never warmed them nor the street cleaner wet them. Illegal posters hung in tatters from the walls, parked mopeds blocked his way, soft-drink cans rolled away from him into hollows in the paving. He'd eaten early, with the workmen. It was still quiet. Metal grills were down over corner shops and from behind half-closed shutters above him came the signature tune of the one-thirty TV news, the cheerful clacking of cutlery, snatches of conversation. He needed the walk to burn off the vin santo and biscuits Lapo had insisted on, and to think things over a bit, if you could call it thinking. Just picturing things, really. A pretty Japanese girl . . .

A sweet little face, Lapo had said, and a trim figure and she liked to dress well, not showily but well. And that was the marshal's problem . . . She came from Tokyo too, like Issino, but from a well-to-do middle-class family who had sent her to Florence to prepare her doctorate in art history. She had returned home after the first three months, told her parents what she had really been spending her time on and then come back against their wishes and without their support.

She had paid Peruzzi for her apprenticeship and, after that, had lived frugally for a year, sleeping behind the workshop and eating a sandwich, at her bench or in some square or park. More recently, she had been producing finished work for Peruzzi and was living in a little place of her own. When the marshal had been perplexed by her leaving a good family, a comfortable life and a respectable, dignified line of study, suitable for an intelligent young woman, Lapo had shaken his head. Akiko couldn't stick the life her parents desired for her. She had always been a tomboy and wanted to work with her hands. The family was very conservative. Her older sister had been married off to a businessman in an arranged match and was dying of boredom in a fancy house with two small children in the country, miles from Tokyo. Her husband worked in the city and appeared when it suited him, usually tumbling drunk from a taxi after midnight. Lapo reckoned Akiko had the right idea:

—She wanted out. She hated Tokyo and she loved it here, so why not? She wasn't just learning a craft, she was learning the business. Peruzzi exports to Tokyo, you know, exclusively to one shop. We all thought she'd have taken over managing the workshop one day—not that Peruzzi would ever retire but ever since the heart attack . . . well, you can imagine it's been on his mind.

—Of course . . . and he hasn't your luck, I mean, no children? I thought he mentioned a son, once . . . that time when there was the business of his car being burned. Now I think about it, I could have sworn Lorenzini said he was so relieved it was the son who came to us to do the report for the insurance company.

—It would have been. He does a lot for his father but it doesn't include learning to make shoes. He's an accountant and a successful one. Done very well for himself. Peruzzi's face turns pink with pride at the mention of his name, worships the ground he walks on because he went to university. Are you going to have a coffee and wait for him? He'll be back from the hospital any time.

—No, no . . . I'll come back another time. Remember, not a word to anyone.

—Don't you worry about that.

But why that odd look? Was it a look that said 'You're not one of us'? A look that shut him out? If it was, then this was going to be a difficult case. Lapo talked on because he was a talker but he wasn't his usual self. His voice had been subdued:

—Can you be sure it's her you've found? That she didn't just go off? Sorry . . . you'd know, of course. Only, we all thought she'd gone to Rome. She had a friend there. Peruzzi said that was bound to be where she'd gone. Anyway, I'm not going to talk to anybody about this, you can rely on me, and Akiko was

93

very discreet herself. She never talked about her private life, she wasn't that sort, so you don't need to worry. None of us knew anything about anything until she'd gone and Peruzzi was so upset—if we had we'd have been pleased for her, pleased to think she'd be staying with us. We were fond of her. Anyway, as I say, you don't need to worry about me saying anything. I'm sure you'll do your duty, whatever happened. Poor Peruzzi. His heart attack and now this. He said there'd been a row though he didn't say what about. Nobody dares mention her name since she disappeared. He had big plans for Akiko. Of course, this puts a different light on the matter. What a nasty mess, especially for you. You've got to deal with it and it could get very unpleasant.

—It's my job.

But Lapo was right. He wasn't looking forward to dealing with this. He liked these people, even the ferocious Peruzzi. Admired him, anyway. And Lapo, if you could keep him off politics, was a good soul. He had seemed distressed, or, at least, ill at ease:

—What is it they say, Marshal? Until you've eaten a kilo of salt with a man, you don't know him. Poor little Akiko. I can't quite believe it, even now.

There was no mistaking that he'd been relieved when the marshal got up to go.

As he walked, he puzzled over those

94

expensive clothes . . . Peruzzi was always difficult to deal with but if he'd been letting his apprentices live in he'd have something to hide. He was also deeply upset about the girl and it looked as though he was about to be even more upset when the marshal approached him about what had happened to her. There was no doubt that the shoe was hers. The first finished shoes she'd ever made, Lapo said. The reason why they looked patchy was that they were made from leftover scraps of leather. That also explained the lack of a maker's name. She'd been very proud of them. Her belt did have the maker's name, though. A distressed Peruzzi with something to hide and another heart attack waiting to happen was going to need careful planning, very careful . . .

So, those expensive clothes . . .

Of course, if Peruzzi was paying for them, it didn't necessarily mean . . .

These things happen. Men of sixty-odd, even seventy-odd, who'd set up house at the usual age, been content with a humdrum marriage, taken by surprise by a belated passion. The marshal had seen a few of them in his time, families broken up, businesses or careers in the army or in government ruined.

Later, in his office, talking it over with Lorenzini, he was moved to complain again, 'What is the matter with everybody?'

'Who do you mean, everybody?'

'Well, Peruzzi—if it was Peruzzi—and if it

wasn't, then it was still somebody, wasn't it? Some rich man making a fool of himself, spending money on that young woman, and Esposito, too—if we can believe Di Nuccio wrecking his career, and . . .'

'And?'

And the captain. Better not mention that one.

Lorenzini waited for the rest and when it didn't come, he said, 'Must be the spring.'

'It's summer by now,' returned the marshal crossly.

*　　*　　*

It was summer. Summer uniform and shirtsleeves in the office. That was a relief because the heat continued excessive for June. The builders were clearing out and that was an even bigger relief. But on Friday afternoon Lorenzini put his head in at the marshal's door looking worried.

'What's the matter?'

'I think you should come up and see.'

'Have they finished or haven't they?'

'Oh, yes. They have finished.'

As they climbed the stairs to the dormitories, the marshal grumbled, 'I asked you to keep an eye . . . I can't be everywhere.'

'No. It's just that the last few days . . . We're a man short now, remember, and I can't be everywhere either. I go home at night, so . . .

Besides, the structural work looked all right. I checked . . .'

'Well, then? What's the problem?'

'Just the tiles.'

'The tiles? What the devil do the tiles matter—as long as they were cheap!'

'They were cheap . . . and we agreed they should do the wall in the kitchen, behind the cooker, as well . . .'

Lorenzini stood back to let the marshal go into the bright new bathroom. He practically exploded.

*   *   *

'Pink?' Captain Maestrangelo wasn't one for exploding but the marshal could imagine him on the other end of the line, his face dark with annoyance. 'Pink?'

'Yes.'

'And you're telling me nobody noticed?'

'They've been using the toilet down here. They had to tile the floor before they could put the new one in up there.'

'For God's sake, your men were getting water from there in buckets. You told me so.'

'No, from the kitchen. It was easier.'

'But you said the kitchen's pink as well!'

'Only one wall and that was the last thing they did, this morning.'

'And what excuse did they give?'

'None. The budget was what it was. Nobody

specified anything except that they should be the cheapest available. It was a job lot of seconds.'

'So they're faulty as well?'

'Nothing you can see.'

'You can just see that they're pink! How pink? Pale? Quiet?'

'No.'

'Oh, God . . . The general will have to be told.'

'Yes.'

'It's not appropriate, not appropriate at all.'

'No.'

*   *   *

Church bells were ringing. Warm laurel bushes perfumed the morning air coming in at the open window. Whenever he had a problem to work on, Sunday morning was the time for it. The small, tinny church bells spoke of quiet streets where only the bars selling fresh cakes remained open, ready to parcel up glazed apple tart in fancy paper and trailing gold ribbon to take to gran's for Sunday dinner after Mass. The dominant cathedral bells spoke of a mixture of churchgoers in Sunday clothes and tourists with bare red shoulders hung with cameras. Smells of incense, sun cream, beeswax, hot dogs, perfume and pizza by the slice. The criminal fraternity could be assumed to be sleeping in and the marshal's desk was as clear as his conscience.

What was her name again? He had to look in his notebook. Akiko. Lapo hadn't known her surname. He scanned his scribbled notes. Pretty as a Japanese doll, intelligent, tough. Gave up family, financial security, presumably friends back home. Followed her own path. Self-confessed tomboy. Wanted to work with her hands. So . . . he closed the notebook . . . she had fetched up on the left bank of the Arno among the Florentine artisans in a tiny square with no real name. An odd thing that Lapo had told him the other day was that one of the little side streets right there had once been known as Japanese Corner, but that was five hundred years or so ago and nobody seemed to remember exactly why there were so many Japanese here then.

Occasionally she ate a good meal at Lapo's but most days she ate at her bench, if it was raining, chatting in Japanese to Issino, or took her sandwich and went for a walk to get a bit of exercise. The marshal was forced to admit to himself that, whatever had happened to the Japanese girl, he had mentally absolved the apprentice of any involvement in it. He was so . . . contained, so correct, so innocent in his attitude. That had to be wrong. That was, practically speaking, racist and he mustn't act on it. He must ignore that impression and enquire into his movements in the same way as into Peruzzi's. The trouble was, he felt rather the same way about Peruzzi. His instinct told him that Peruzzi had never been guilty of anything worse than a sharp temper and a tendency to drive people out of his shop, refusing to sell them anything if he didn't like them. A tendency he shared with countless other artisans in the city. It was understandable, if you thought about it. What was less understandable was the girl's story. He went over it again in his head. That arranged marriage of her sister's . . . she liked it here and she wanted out . . . why not? Well, why not? Because something was wrong. Something didn't fit. It was difficult to get at exactly what it was because he kept on being distracted by cultural differences. Now, that was no good. He just didn't believe it would help because, surely, the things that mattered were the things that made all people the same, like greed, selfishness, jealousy. Sex and money, money and sex . . . Cultural backgrounds only provided different dressing for the same thing.

'No, no . . .' He spoke suddenly aloud and got up to walk over to his map and put his finger on the little nameless square. Then he walked to the window and parked himself there.

No. Because a freethinking, parent-defying tomboy who wants to learn to work with her hands and make her own way in life does not want a sugar daddy who buys her expensive clothes. At that rate she would hardly have lived for a year behind the workshop and the clothes themselves would have been different. Not navy-blue linen. And not those plain white cotton knickers from a department store, either.

'No, no . . .'

Peruzzi? No. Whatever the sleeping arrangements might be behind the workshop, they could hardly be conducive to a clandestine affair. Peruzzi was a widower. He could have taken her home if he'd wanted to. He must have made a small fortune in his time and never left his last long enough to spend any of it. Of course, a man of his age might feel a bit foolish, falling for such a young woman. But when did Peruzzi ever care a damn what anybody thought? Unless the fright of his illness had changed him completely. No, no . . . Whatever his faults, Peruzzi wasn't capable of hypocrisy. A little place of her own, Lapo had said. Peruzzi might be paying for that. No, no . . .

He stood at the open window for a long time, breathing the morning air, staring down at the laurel bushes without seeing them. What was he doing? A young woman was dead and he was trying to exonerate two obvious suspects before even having questioned them. Well, he had until tomorrow to pull himself together. In the meantime, the laurel-scented air was now carrying wafts of bacon and tomato sauce to him. The lads upstairs, pink tiles or no pink tiles, must be happily cooking up mountains of pasta in their freshly painted kitchen and he himself was looking forward to roast rabbit. He looked at his watch. Teresa wouldn't add that final splash of wine until he was changing out of his uniform. He closed the window.

Teresa always liked to lay the table in the dining room on Sundays though she no longer used her mother's handmade lace cloth, saying she couldn't get it laundered in Florence. At home in Sicily it had been sent to the nuns who cared for the altar cloths. Today there was a glossy green cloth. There was also an ominous silence. He placed an open bottle of wine on its silver coaster and looked at the boys. Giovanni gazed up at him, his big brown eyes full of apprehension.

'All right, son?'

He only bit his lip and lowered his gaze. Had they been quarrelling? If they had, Teresa had clearly put a stop to it. And, by the look on 'Totò's face, he'd got the worst of his mother's telling off. Surely he hadn't been crying? He didn't cry easily, unlike Giovanni, because he was fiercely proud. When he did, it was usually more in anger than in sorrow.

Nothing was said about whatever it was and the marshal remained lost in his meanderings about artisans and foreigners, and whether they should go to Lapo's for Giovanni's birthday. They ate ravioli stuffed with ricotta and spinach, and Teresa gave his a sprinkling of grated cheese and black pepper. No butter.

Afterwards, she came in with a huge oval dish of roasted rabbit joints in a herb-scented gravy surrounded by crisp little roast potatoes. 'Ah . . .'

Totò jumped up from his seat.

'Totò!' Teresa's tone made it clear that whatever it was had already been dealt with and that she was in no mood for any more of it. 'Sit down, please. You can eat some potatoes and a green salad.'

'No, I can't! I've told you I can't! How can I eat anything with a dead animal lying on the table? I'd be sick! It's disgusting!' He shot out of the room, crying.

Giovanni gazed from one parent to the other, his brown eyes eloquent of a soul torn between distress for his brother and hunger for Sunday roast.

His mother started to serve him.

'Pass me your plate, too, will you, Salva. This serving dish is too hot to move.'

'I can do that. Don't you want to go and get Totò?'

'No. He's best left alone for now. I'll give him something to eat later.'

And, though Teresa had never tolerated finicky eating or bad manners at the table, her tone was quiet, even tender.

Well, she wouldn't want him interfering.

She'd said a few times lately:
—Don't say anything to him, Salva. Promise me.
So he kept quiet. Giovanni was watching, waiting for a sign. They, at least, understood each other. He smiled at him and they tucked in.

That night, when he was in bed and Teresa was putting a refill in the mosquito killer, he ventured to ask, 'Did he eat some supper, at least?'

'Some yoghurt and cereal.'

'Yoghurt . . . ? He's a growing boy, for God's sake! Not only that but half the world's children are starving while he's complaining—'

'Salva.'

'But it's true.'

'I know it's true. Please don't say anything to him. You promised me, remember.'

'Have I said a word? Have I?'

'No.'

'I know what my mother would have done.'

'No, you don't.'

'Of course I do! She'd have given me a good hiding if I'd dared to behave like that!'

'No, she wouldn't.'

'She'd have given me a good hiding, I'm telling you.'

'How many times in your life did your mother ever give you a good hiding?'

He lay there a moment, thinking it over, then admitted, 'Only once, that I can

104

remember . . . but that's only because I would never have dared—'

'So what had you done?'

'Eh? Oh . . . I forget.'

'Go on, what?'

'I've just said, I forget.'

'It's funny, isn't it? People have confessed murder to you, plenty of times, but nobody ever confesses to wetting the bed.'

'I didn't wet the bed!'

'I didn't say you did. I'm just saying that people confess monstrous crimes but not little embarrassments.' She got into bed and switched the bedside lamp off. 'I suppose it had something to do with food.'

Under cover of darkness he admitted, 'I stole Nunziata's birthday chocolates . . . and ate some of them.'

'How many of them?'

'What does it matter how many? Stealing's stealing, isn't it?'

'How many?'

Silence. Then, very quietly: 'All of them.'

'I thought so. Leave Totò to me, Salva. Poor little thing. He's in love.'

'Oh, no! Oh, please! Not him, too! For God's sake, Teresa, he's a child!'

'A teenager. And keep calm.'

'I am calm!'

'Sh . . .' Her arm slid over his chest. 'She's in his class and she's very pretty. I've seen her.'

'Hmph.'

'Her father's Sicilian and her mother's Danish. She has the most beautiful long blonde curls and dark eyes.'

'And she's a vegetarian. I suppose.'

'And she's a vegetarian.' She kissed his cheek and whispered, 'You went on a diet for me once upon a time, if you remember.'

He turned to her in the dark with a sort of sorrowful tenderness and murmured, 'I go on a diet for you practically every day.'

*   *   *

The next day, in excellent spirits, he sailed through a morning in court and then tackled the problem of Peruzzi.

There was a couple in the workshop. Foreigners, you could see that. They were big and heavy, and the woman's bare arms were roasted red. They had their backs to Peruzzi whose gimlet eye looked murderous.

'If you go to my shop in Borgo San Jacopo, you'll find more choice there and an assistant to help you!'

This was ignored, no doubt because they didn't understand a word of it.

The woman had picked a shoe out of the window and now she put it on the floor and drew back the linen curtain to reach in for another. Her husband was busy with a pocket calculator. They looked at the results of his calculations and spoke for a moment in their own language. Then she dropped the second shoe on the floor and they walked out without a word.

Peruzzi's face was purple.

'Did you see that? Like they're in a supermarket! They come in here without a word to me and stand two feet away from me discussing my shoes as though I didn't exist. And then the calculator. They all do it—and you can bet they're wondering how it is that my shoes cost more than the factory-made rubbish they see at home. Thank you and good-morning. A pleasure to have met you!' He slammed the door and locked it. Outside, the couple were unfolding a map, oblivious. Peruzzi went back to his last, muttering fiercely. The marshal was pretty sure he caught the word 'flame-thrower' and thought to himself that Peruzzi hardly needed one. The tiny workshop vibrated with his burning anger.

'Steady on . . .' he dared to say. 'Your health's more important . . . Couldn't you just keep your door shut?'

'It's hot, damn it!' He got up and wrenched it open. Then he turned his angry eyes on the marshal. 'And you don't need to tell me what you're here for, either!' He wagged his large hand in the marshal's face. 'I've nothing more to say about it! If she's not in Rome I don't know where she is! She could have gone back to Tokyo for all I know—and if you've got the time to be running round after youngsters who don't know their own minds, I haven't! All right?'

The marshal stood his ground, his face expressionless, but anger seemed to rebound from the walls of the little room and all his carefully prepared preliminaries were clearly useless. Lapo must have talked, though without telling all.

'Can we sit down a minute?' He spoke very quietly in the hope of defusing the situation.

'Look, I've said already she had a friend in Rome! That's all I know! How many more of you do I have to say it to before you all leave me in peace?'

'Peruzzi, sit down, will you. I know, partly anyway, what happened to your other apprentice, the Japanese girl. I need to talk to you. It's important and you might well find it upsetting, so please, let's sit down.'

He saw the anger drain from Peruzzi's face and at once regretted its going. Despite his height, his wiriness and his big bony face, he looked old and vulnerable all of a sudden, without his prickly shell. It crossed the marshal's mind that if he took the news really badly, which he well might, he wouldn't recover. If, instead of his old bristly self, he should become a pathetic invalid . . .

Still, there was no going back. What could he do? He persuaded him to sit down and then he told him.

He didn't look at Peruzzi as he talked, but

sitting beside him on the smooth old bench he felt every catch in his breath, every increase of tension in his wiry frame. Beyond the half-drawn linen curtain people were going about their business. Lapo's head passed by above his hedge, a motorino was heard revving up. An invisible someone called down from a high window to an upturned face below. But it was all like something happening in another dimension, like on television with the sound turned low. He couldn't avoid admitting that the girl's face was unrecognisable but he didn't say why, didn't say there was no face. Or hands. The hands that would have talked to Forli would have talked to Peruzzi, too. He'd taught them what they knew and that must be important to him. Well, he wasn't going to say anything about the fish in the pool, not when he was convinced he could hear Peruzzi's heart pounding. Talk steadily, quietly, taking the longest way round, giving him time to take it in bit by bit . . . could an ambulance get into the tiny square, if . . .? The approaches were so narrow it would surely scrape the walls if it got through at all. He was so tense, so silent. One of his outbursts of rage, being more familiar, would be less alarming. How long was it since the operation? Perhaps he needn't say yet that he was talking about murder. Peruzzi was sharp, he might understand, ask. Don't tell him everything, no need for that. The smooth old bench, the gloom, the seclusion from the rest behind the curtain, the leathery smell of the kneeler . . . Don't tell everything . . .

—Forgive me, Father, for I have sinned . . .

Had he ever confessed about the chocolates? Was it before or after his first confession? In any case, it was always a problem, that horrible feeling of shame that never seemed to attach itself to any particular event, so he always used to make his sins up.

—I have been disobedient to my father three times and to my mother four times . . .

Juggling the numbers each week. The curtain had been thick, rough, velvety stuff, dark red . . .

Talk to him about her quietly, things learned from Lapo. Keep talking of good things about her until he joins in. If he talks he'll have to breathe properly.

The door always used to creak as you pushed your way out of the darkness to the candlelight. Then the priest, old and cross, would grasp at the dark curtain with a gnarled hand and peer out at you, checking who'd been and who hadn't . . .

Only tell him what's really necessary. Details can wait for another day.

Peruzzi's head dropped into his hands and he rubbed at his eyes, then turned and interrupted. 'How can you be sure? If you say she . . . if her face—how can you be sure? There are dozens of Japanese tourists in town . . .'

'But you know, do you, where she went to eat her sandwich and take a stroll to stretch her legs.'

'Sitting at a last all day . . . I ought to have done the same and maybe I wouldn't be in this state now . . .'

'Did you ever go with her?'

'No. No, I've always liked a good meal and five minutes with the paper. No, I never . . .' He was staring out of the show window but without seeing anything. He got up and drew the linen curtain closed, then sat down again. His face was very white, with blue shadows round the lips.

The marshal went on, gentle, watchful, 'But still, you know the places where she went, perhaps? Does the place I described to you sound likely?'

'She told me she just walked around until she found somewhere quiet. A garden, a fountain in a square . . . getting to know Florence, she said. Not the Boboli Gardens so often because you have to pay—you can't be sure, can you? Not if her face . . .'

In silence, the marshal offered him the shoe. He didn't recoil as the nervous apprentice had done. He took it into his large hand, which almost enveloped it, and ran his fingers over the stitching as if he could read it like braille.

'We'll still need a formal identification—'

'She learned in a year what took me five.'

111

Still his bony, work-scarred fingers were reading the shoe, seam by seam. The marshal couldn't take his eyes from this process. 'She had a different way of learning things, you see, not like ours. Not just repetition, not trial and error.' His fingers read on but he didn't look down at the shoe. 'Right from the start, if something didn't come out right she'd make me show her again and then she'd sit still for a long, long time, thinking. Then she'd do it again and it would be right. Not perfect, and not quick, either, but right. Of course, she has brains, that's the difference. She has brains . . .'

'We must inform her parents if you have an address.' He didn't know which would be worse, to show that ravaged skull to her parents or to Peruzzi. He still hadn't understood what their real relationship had been and besides, the last thing he needed now was to have Peruzzi clam up on him because of letting the apprentices live in. He trod carefully. He didn't much like the look of that blueness round the lips. He didn't like that at all. He would ask for her address and her parents' address, too. They were bound to get her DNA from something in her flat. He didn't take his eyes off the shoemaker, who was still staring at nothing as his fingers contacted her through the stitching of the little shoe. What should he do? In his head he asked Captain Maestrangelo, who would surely know In his head, came the captain's answer:

112

'Follow your instinct. You decide. You know your people.

Earth, air, fire, water, and the Florentines . . .

What did it mean, after all? Sitting beside him was a man, growing old, who had invested something of himself the marshal didn't know quite what, in this young foreigner.

'If only she'd been willing to marry. She always swore she wouldn't but I thought that with the baby . . . then she would have stayed. She said she was so happy here but you never know, you see, whether one day her own country, her own people . . . you never know. A baby would have made a difference, wouldn't it?' He turned and looked into the marshal's eyes searching for an answer.

'Yes, I'm sure it would have made a difference.'

Peruzzi looked down at the shoe as if seeing it for the first time. He turned it over and examined it for faults, then ran his hand round the edge of the sole. 'The first layer is leather, the second rubber, the third leather again. Waterproof. But she put this little stick-on rubber sole anyway. You see, she wanted them to last for ever because they were her first.' He smiled at the thought, then fell silent and stared into space again.

Follow your instinct. That was all very well but whatever unreasonable hopes Peruzzi might have had—and he wouldn't be the first —what, in heaven's name, had the Japanese girl been thinking about? She wouldn't be the first either, if she'd wanted to make a fool of an old man. No, no . . . nothing about that idea was right. She was learning a trade, a skill from him. She would have admired him for what he could teach her, of course, and there was no accounting for what women found attractive— And she was pregnant, after all, but—

He was going to need a DNA sample from Peruzzi in case there was evidence that he'd been in her flat. Well, he wasn't going to ask for that today.

He scanned Peruzzi's face. His colour seemed slightly better. 'How are you feeling? This has been a shock, I know, and you have to be careful.'

Try as he might, he just couldn't see it. But who paid for the clothes if not Peruzzi? Who? Why not just ask him? 'Peruzzi? You've said she was a pretty young woman and I hear from your neighbours around here—who seemed to be fond of her—that she liked to dress well.'

'She has taste, very refined . . .'

'Yes, but fine clothes are expensive and I gather she had very little money so I can't help asking who paid for them . . .'

'She buys them herself. Her family has money—he probably told you that—but she won't ask them for anything, anything at all.'

So, the only thing Lapo hadn't gossiped about was her death—and that was probably

114

only out of fear for Peruzzi's damaged heart. Blast the man. He wouldn't have believed it of him.

Peruzzi breathed a deep, shaky sigh. He set the shoe down on the carpeted floor. 'I thought the baby would settle it, I really did. I could have done a lot for them. We had plans. Did he tell you about that?'

'About her taking over here, one day? Yes.'

'Who would have thought when she trotted off that sunny morning . . . she was so alive . . .'

In relinquishing the small shoe he had let go of its owner. That was the first time he had recognised that she was gone, used the past tense.

'I could have done so much . . . No more than she deserved, mind you. She had talent and she had character. It was a privilege to have taught her. I don't know if that makes any sense to you.'

'It does, yes. Anyone with a skill like yours would want to pass it on. It's only natural. And I gather your own son's talents lie in another direction.'

Just as Lapo had said, Peruzzi's face flushed with pleasure. He didn't actually smile but his eyes lit up. 'My son went to university and studied Economics and Commerce. He's an accountant.'

'So I heard, and a successful one, too, I gather.'

'He's doing very well.' Thank heaven, he

was looking better. The blueness round his lips had faded. His son had to be more important, surely. He would survive this. He was beginning to look almost normal. 'I never have to fill in a tax form or worry about a thing. It's a godsend. He's been very good to me, especially since his mother died.'

'You're very lucky—I hate all that sort of thing myself. Listen, Peruzzi'—he looked so much better that the marshal decided to risk it —'I've kept you from your work and, sorry as I am to have been the one to bring you bad news, I need your help. I'm pretty sure that her death . . . that it wasn't an accident. I have to find out what happened and before that I need to identify her beyond doubt. I need the address of her flat and her parents' address, too.'

Peruzzi turned his head and focused on the marshal's face, sharp eyes glittering, himself again. 'Not an accident. So that's the way the wind blows, is it? Well, you've a job on your hands and it's not going to be easy, I appreciate that. All I'll say is this: nothing can bring her back—I don't understand why it had to end up like this but nothing can bring her back. So any journalists who show their faces around here will wish they hadn't! I, for one, shan't be saying another word.'

He got to his feet and went over to a corner where, from a desk cluttered with receipts and notes, he produced a visiting card. 'This is her

116

parents' address—oh, don't worry, it's in normal writing on the back. Her flat's in via del Leone near the corner of the piazza there, second floor. I'll write it down for you.'

As he handed over a scrap of paper and the Japanese visiting card, Issino appeared from a door behind him. He was carrying a stack of shoeboxes. 'Everything OK . . .' he began, then stopped, looking from the marshal to Peruzzi, alarmed.

The marshal stood up and put a big hand on the apprentice's shoulder. 'It's all right. You're not in any trouble. Do you understand that?'

'Yes. Thank you.' But his gaze was fixed on Peruzzi.

Well, Peruzzi's arrangements with his apprentice, like his DNA, must wait for another day. He wasn't going anywhere. Another heart attack was the last thing anybody needed.

As he opened the door for the marshal, Peruzzi said, 'You know, you'll say I'm past it and I'd be the first to admit I'm not the romantic sort, but I'd have sworn she was in love. Not that she ever said much but she wasn't herself those last few days. I caught her crying, once, while she worked. Not a sound, just a tear, fell on her hand. When somebody doesn't talk, you can't help them. No use insisting, might make it worse. Oh, to hell with it! Whether I'm past it or not, I can see what's in front of my eyes. She was in love. And you see, if it happened like you say then I'm right, aren't I? She didn't just walk out. The baby would have kept her, like I said.'

The marshal left.

CHAPTER SIX

Standing at the window in the tiny flat next morning, the marshal felt that all too familiar toad of anxiety squatting in his stomach and there was no dislodging it. The technician from the police lab had left, having lifted fingerprints and collected the contents of the bathroom wastebin with which he had seemed well satisfied. Nail clippings, used tissues, two hairs with root bulbs and a small sticking plaster with blood on it. There might well be evidence of a man's presence. And if it turned out to be Peruzzi? He was very put out but, as often happens, he couldn't put his finger on the root cause. So he stood there, staring out at the rain-washed morning street. The excessive heat had culminated in a heavy rainstorm during the night, which had cleared the air if not the marshal's head. He was trying to remember the name of the people in the flat opposite, a very few metres away. He couldn't. He might be no great thinker, but his memory usually served him pretty well and this failure added irritation to his discomfort. A good many years had passed, of course, but in an old-fashioned corner like this one, things don't change that fast so, when he'd looked at the Japanese girl's address, scribbled on bit of paper by Peruzzi, he'd been pleased. He was at home around here with Nardi and his two women and the butcher's shop where they had fought. And though Franco was gone, which was a great pity, the butcher with the shiny pink face would surely tell him something.

The fancied-up bar would be a waste of time, he'd known that, but you have to be thorough so he'd gone in anyway, and asked if they knew the Japanese girl.

—Have you got a photo of her?

—No. She lived right there.

—I haven't been working here long but I don't think she ever came in . . .

I'm not surprised, the marshal had thought, with a black look at the dishes of congealed lasagne waiting to be heated up. In the old days he'd have had a coffee with Franco, who would have known every move she had ever made whether she went in or not.

The butcher, pink and smiling as ever, did know her:

—Very precise. Likes to cook pork but always has it minced. Not keen on beal.

—Beal?

—Couldn't say her 'v's.

—What about a man in her life?

—Definitely. Italian, too, but likes his Japanese food, or so she says. No, we've never seen him, but then he probably comes round in the evenings or on the weekends and we live out in the country, so . . . We haven't seen her in a week or two—I hope she's not in trouble?

120

She's not here illegally, is she? I can't believe that. I mean, she's so precise and organised.

—Yes.

So this little flat was no surprise, as far as the way she kept it was concerned. Simple, clean and neat. A pale-blue silk counterpane on a single bed, one plant, dead now, white shelves with art books, a white table and chair.

The flat itself, though . . . It must be five, six years since he'd last set foot there. It was impossible to connect this freshly painted space with the dark hole without heating or sanitation in which Clementina had died. The old lavatory out on the staircase was now a storage cupboard full of spare tiles and cans of paint. He eventually worked out that what had been a very small kitchen with a tiny high window was now a cooking alcove and a tiny bathroom. There were radiators. He was willing to bet that the rent was extremely high. Franco would have known. The butcher didn't, but he did say that the place had stood empty for years because the woman who inherited it was bankrupt—couldn't sell and no money to do it up—but it must have changed hands recently and now Akiko was the first tenant. He also said that if things went on like this there wouldn't be a Florentine left in the area.

If he were to be absolutely honest, the marshal would have to admit that he chose that moment to distract him from a Lapo-style political diatribe to tell him what had happened to the Japanese girl:

—No!

—I'm afraid so. You're sure you never saw her with anybody?

—No, never. She was always so lively and busy—she never walked anywhere, always trotted . . . pretty, too. Very pretty. She was learning to make shoes, you know. I remember her showing the wife—wait a minute—Lucia!

—What's to do?

—Come out here a minute!

—What's the matter? I've these five chickens to dress before . . . Oh, Marshal! Let me wipe my hands. How are you? And your wife? Did she ever learn to drive?

—Yes, she did. Not from me, though.

—Lucia, listen: the marshal's here about Akiko. She's dead and he thinks she was murdered.

—No! Our little Akiko? No! Whoever would want to do a thing like that?

—That's what he's trying to find out. They found her in the Boboli Gardens, can you imagine? You talked to her more than I did. You remember those shoes?

—Her patchwork shoes! She was so proud of them, patchy or not, and she dressed really well. Such a trim little figure. If only I had that tiny waistline but I've been like this ever since I had my third.

But she'd never seen Akiko with a man and didn't know who paid for the fine clothes.

122

—I do know she always had to be very careful with her money, though. She said so. That tiny old flat of Clementina's was the cheapest she could find but it was expensive, she said, for what it was.

—She didn't say how much?

—No. Only that it was more than she could really afford.

Before he'd left the brightly lit butcher's shop, where he couldn't help noticing that a hanging side of beef was dripping blood on to pink marbled tiles, Nardi's name had come up:

—My man Lorenzini's trying to talk some sense into Monica, get her to drop the case.

—He'd better go to the club on the twenty-third, then.

—Why's that?

—Nardi's singing. It's a special party. Night before San Giovanni. Monica's intending to be there and so is Costanza. They say it'll end in bloodshed.

—Oh, Lord . . .

Now, what the devil was the name of the chap on the first floor opposite? Beppe . . . Peppe—Pippo! That was it. A scrap of satisfaction on a day that seemed to be falling apart. Every time he thought he had a hold of something in this case, it slipped through his fingers. Starting with that awful woman who'd left her handbag by the pool. The dress shop, too, where that expensive sweater had come from. He should have insisted, sent someone to go through the books in case of a credit card payment, whether the woman was in a crisis or not. This was a murder, for heaven's sake. But you can't force people to help you . . . the poor woman wasn't a suspect so what was he supposed to do? Get a warrant? No, no . . . that sort of thing didn't do any good. People had to want to help, otherwise . . . he was sure she'd been concerned . . .

And what about that missing second shoe? He'd had two men search for it, especially in the wooded patch over the wall where they'd run the pool water, since you can't hide much in a small formal garden. They'd found nothing, anyway. And it wasn't in the water. Nobody would go trailing through the gardens carrying the shoe of a murder victim, would they? A dog might run off with it, but dogs weren't allowed in.

And yesterday? There was no avoiding it: yesterday, he should have questioned Issino before talking to Peruzzi. Follow your instinct was very fine advice but things have to be done in the proper way, even so. The proper way was not to let two possible suspects . . . no. Yes! To let two possible suspects talk things over and agree on a story. You separate them until they've both told their version. Instinct or no instinct, that was what had to be done

The window where the marshal stood staring out was a small french window with no balcony outside but with a low railing to prevent anyone falling to the narrow paved street below. Clementina had stood here, practically naked, ranting at Pippo's wife over there and cursing the crowd below. What a scene . . .

He let his mind drift back to that stifling August day, knowing he was avoiding facing up to the one thing about yesterday's mess that was gnawing at him.

If only he'd come away right after talking to Peruzzi, given himself time to think, work things out. It was his annoyance that had led him to mess things up, but Lapo had promised to say nothing and went on swearing he had said nothing in the face of an obvious contradiction:

—Oh, Marshal! When I say a thing I mean it, don't make any mistake about that! Good God, if I'd gossiped about what I know—a story like that would have been on the front page of *La Nazione*! And you think I'd have risked giving Peruzzi another heart attack?

—I realise that. I'm not saying that, but he knew—'

—If he knew she was dead, it wasn't from me—

—Will you listen to me for a minute? All I'm saying was that he was expecting me and he knew what I was there for. He said so in as many words!

—Well, of course he knew! That wouldn't take much working out. He hasn't heard a word for days!

—All right, we'll leave it at that. But while we're on the subject, why don't you tell me, here and now, what was going on with Peruzzi and the Japanese girl. Come on. An indiscretion for an indiscretion. You owe me that.

—There was no indiscretion! All I said was that you'd be coming to see him and that he should be careful. And I was right about that, wasn't I? I've known you for a long time and when I said I was sure you'd do your duty, I meant it.

—So, help me.

—What more do you expect from me? Have I said a word? We all protect our own, Marshal. We both know that. Accuse Peruzzi? No, no. no, no. I wouldn't have thought it of you. Not that I don't appreciate your position but I wouldn't have thought it of you. You'll have to excuse me now. I've got work to do.

He shouldn't have spoken to Lapo. It couldn't have done any good and had probably done some harm.

The marshal leaned his forehead against the glass to look down at two people who had stopped to talk in the wet street directly below. A large woman with two plastic bags of shopping and a boy on a moped. The boy kept revving up, trying to get away from her, but each time she would call out and stop him. Perhaps it was because he wasn't wearing his helmet. The narrow street was filling with blue smoke. The marshal continued to watch the scene playing out below what he still thought of as Clementina's flat, grateful for any distraction from his discomfort.

He had lost Lapo but, what was worse, he had lost the whole square. Again, the thing would have been to separate his witnesses, not let the story get around the square faster than he could get round it himself. But by the time everybody in that tiny space had finished listening in to their altercation from over the hedge—he'd kept his voice down almost to a whisper but Lapo, a real Florentine, could have been heard in Pisa—Peruzzi had come out on his doorstep and so had everybody else.

After that, he had been wasting his time. After that, it had been hear no evil, see no evil, speak no evil. After that, shrugged shoulders, outspread arms, opened palms, silence. He might have been back home in Sicily except that their eyes met his, defiant not shifty, and the few remarks that had been made were worthy of Peruzzi himself.

He was an outcast. And the worst of it was that he felt the same way they did. He couldn't, even now, though he had to be lying about the girl buying those clothes herself, suspect Peruzzi of anything more than a foolish passion.

Separate your witnesses. He didn't want to separate them, dammit! It was their solidarity with each other—and his with them, after all these years—that he counted on. He knew no other way of doing things and it had never failed him before . . .

Pippo's wife, Maria Pia, opened the widow opposite and leaned out to feel at the socks on a washing line stretched below it. She unpegged them, disappeared for a minute, then leaned out to hang a dripping blouse. After a glance at the neighbours' washing and another at the sky, she covered the blouse with a sheet of polythene.

The marshal opened up the window to the clamp, soapy air. 'Good-morning.'

A few minutes later she was in the flat with him, talking over Clementina's story, Franco's long illness and the shocking rent that 'our little Akiko' had to pay for this tiny place. Akiko would never have harmed a fly so why would anyone want to harm her? Maybe this flat brought bad luck, though she didn't believe in that sort of thing herself. She'd had many a conversation with her in the butcher's. All the women were curious to know how she cooked the meat she bought, she was so very particular about how it was cut or minced. Once, Akiko had invited her up here to try something. There had to have been a dozen little bowls of different things—very tasty, she had to say—but no, she'd never tried it herself.

Pippo never fancied foreign food and, besides, so much preparation, chopping all

128

those things. Of course, Akiko was so fast, never walked if she could run.

A man in her life? Oh, yes, there was a man, though she'd only seen him from above, one night when they'd come home together and she'd just been closing the shutters as they unlocked the street door below. Of course, the street lighting around here—they always say they're going to see to it but—anyway, the only thing she could say for sure was that he was very tall. It was true, yes, that Akiko was tiny, but—no, she was sure she remembered him being tall. Oh, she wouldn't like to guess his age. From above and behind, in the dark? No. Just that he was a tall man. Somebody else might have seen him, got a better look. She could ask around when she went down to the shops tomorrow. Akiko was always cheerful and chatty but she was very discreet about her private life. They used to tease her in the butcher's about it because she often bought enough for two people but she never said anything much apart from what she cooked for him. Did the marshal think she'd got involved with somebody who was a bad lot? Well, she must have, mustn't she?

Before she had to get back to put the water on for the pasta, she pointed out a photograph in a silver frame on the white shelves. 'That's her with her sister, alike as two peas with their little tartan kilts and white blouses. That's how they were dressed for school, she told me that.

129

You'd have expected something a bit more Japanese, really, wouldn't you? I remember saying to her, 'You can see right away, even at that age, which one's the tomboy.'

She whispered to him, as he opened the door for her, 'I hope you won't mind me asking but I saw a man with a bag leave in a police car before . . . ?'

And, though he didn't give her much of an answer, he didn't mind her asking at all. Life felt back to normal again.

After she'd gone, the marshal added the photograph in its frame to the things he had already collected: a diary, the address book by the phone, a folder with letters and packets of photographs. He took a quick look through one of the packets, sure he'd find the man he was looking for, but it was all shoes, or details of shoes with notes in Japanese on the back. A second seemed to be nothing but views of Florence so he'd have to go through it all later. Out on the landing, as he was locking up, his phone rang.

'Guarnaccia.'

'I hope I'm not disturbing you. I don't know if it's important or not but you did say to call if I found anything . . .'

The woman from the dress shop.

'It's not that I've remembered anything particular . . . or even found anything, really, but it crossed my mind that—since that sweater was last year's—you ought to check

130

the stock house down via Romana. They buy up what's left at the end of the season from shops like ours and sell it off cheaply. If she went there, they might well know her. It's the sort of place where people rummage and chat. You know what I mean?'

'Yes.'

'It's not much, I'm afraid . . . I'm probably disturbing you for nothing.'

'No, no. You did right to call me and I'm very grateful. Have you finished with your workmen?'

'Oh, don't! They've all gone but it's only luck that you haven't been called in to a murder here—I'm sorry, I shouldn't joke when that poor young woman . . . I hope you find out what happened.'

'I'll find out.'

He went downstairs to the wet street and set out with a determined step for nearby via Romana.

A nice woman who was concerned and wanted to help. A place where people rummage and chat. Life was definitely back to normal. He'd find out.

*   *   *

'I'll be right with you! I will—no! Don't put those there! I've told you a dozen times to pack them in boxes! Nobody wants to look at sweaters in June! I'll be right there!'

131

But she wasn't. She was everywhere but. Every now and then her tousled grey-blonde curls and rattling earrings appeared above a rack of clothes, only to disappear behind teetering piles of folded jeans to protest at an invisible assistant.

'I've told you! There's no point in hanging things together because they're the same colour! Divide them by size, for heaven's sake! This rack's supposed to be forty-two, forty-four and look at this! Look at it! Fifty-two! Is that woman still in that cubicle? Well, stay with her! What have I told you about—?'

Suddenly the curls and earrings bounced up by the marshal's shoulder, and the voice cut to a stage whisper as audible as her yells. 'You can see how I'm fixed—you can't imagine how much stuff gets stolen from me in all this chaos but I can't find a decent girl to help me—this one's willing enough but she hasn't the sense she was born with. She's Romanian and, if you ask me, she doesn't understand a word—' She broke off and turned up the volume: 'Put those bikinis back in that box! If you leave them scattered all over the counter like that there won't be one left by the time we shut—not that box! Can't you see I've written "scarves" on the side with a black marker—on the other side, the other side—I know there are belts in it, I know that. That's not your problem. Just put the bikinis in the box they came out of! I think it says bras. Either that or accessories . . .'

132

Red nails clutched at the marshal's black sleeve and the whisper this time was almost a growl. 'You can see how I'm fixed. I can't leave people trying stuff on and if I stay down near the cubicle, people come in and take things. I'm always saying you've got to have order, it's the only way. You'll have to give me some advice. D'you think I should install those whatsit cameras or will I not be able to afford it? She's left that woman on her own again and she's got at least four linen jackets in there. You've got to have order—I'll be right with you. Stay there.'

The marshal stayed, obedient as a well-trained bulldog, the sole solid, stationary clement in a boiling sea of rummaging customers, shifting clothes racks and sliding piles. The only time he moved at all was when a tough-looking young woman rammed him with a rack of glittery frocks.

He glanced at his watch. A quarter to one. With any luck things would quieten down soon and she would surely close, anyway, at one.

Things didn't quieten down. There was more of a crescendo of noise and muddle culminating in the protesting customers being physically evicted and the door locked.

'I've got to talk to the marshal . . . For goodness' sake!'

When they'd all gone, she wiped her brow on a loose, flowery sleeve and said, 'You can see how I'm fixed. You'll have to give me some

133

advice—I mean, just look at that damp patch, up there to the left of the door. I've already had it fixed twice and it's back again. You could probably recommend a reliable builder, somebody in your position, you'd know the right sort . . . I'm exhausted with it all, I can tell you. Let's sit down. This is supposed to be my desk and just look at it . . . Put that stuff anywhere—oh! Give me that silk frock. I've been looking for that for two days. It's to go to the tailor to be shortened . . . have I lost the measurements? I have. There was a little yellow stick-on thing . . .'

'Is this it?' It was stuck to his sleeve.

'Well, thank goodness for that. I could do with somebody like you working for me. I don't think that girl speaks a word of Italian . . . not that she's said anything but . . .'

She wound down after a while, like clockwork. The marshal, watching as the curls and earrings settled, wondered how old she might be. As old as, or older than, himself, probably, but the disorderly mop of curls, her plumpness and the room full of tumbled dresses in which frills and glitter were a dominant theme made her seem like an overtired child who would never get round to putting away her toys and dressing-up clothes.

He gave her some advice in the gravest of tones and she drank it in with equal solemnity. He could just see her telling her favourite customers about it:

134

—The marshal from the Pitti came here and he said to me . . .

And life would tumble along as before.

It turned out that the Japanese girl was a favourite customer. Not that she had a lot to spend but she was so pretty and trim and, of course, size forty—well, there's always plenty of choice in a size that small, including model samples. She remembered that linen sweater, a lovely piece but it didn't sell. Akiko had fished it out from under a pile of dark stuff.

—Most people like something more cheerful, you know, in the summer, especially for the seaside, but you could never get her to buy anything sexy or glamorous even though she'd have looked lovely . . .

—Being that size, she could buy a lot of the big designer stuff, Valentino, Ferré and so on, from the market in Piazza Santo Spirito on Wednesdays. They cut the labels and you get it for practically nothing . . .

This was all music to the marshal's ears since it exonerated Peruzzi from having lied and, perhaps, from everything . . .

—I was sure she was in love. A baby would have made a difference, wouldn't it?

Perhaps not from everything. He'd better ask.

'Oh, yes, there was a man in her life all right, because she brought him to Domani, next door, and that was how she noticed this shop and started coming here.'

'Domani?'

'Domani. The Japanese restaurant next door. You wouldn't have noticed it with the shutter down. It's his closing day. Come back tomorrow. They'll know all about her man. And then, when you've time, you'll come back and see me again, right? Give me some more good advice. Wait a minute while I unlock the door for you . . . It's right, what you said about lining up the racks so I can see to the other end of the room when I'm down here. It's like you say, you've got to have order.'

'That's right. Thank you for your help.'

So . . . Home to a good meal and, this afternoon, a thorough look through the stuff he'd taken from the flat, secure in the knowledge that the Japanese restaurant would provide what he might not find. The shops all had their shutters down and from above his head came the sound of the news and wafts of good dinners. Steam was rising from the road. He kept close to the wall away from the hot sun. In Piazza San Felice the nuns were ushering small children out of the infant school to their waiting parents. Droves of older children were coming towards him from the middle school in Piazza Pitti, so his own two were probably home by now

But if Giovanni was at home, Totò certainly wasn't. As he reached the big piazza, the marshal saw his son, not crossing over to the Pitti and home but bouncing towards him, his face alight, and he was calling out, 'Where were you?'

The marshal stopped in his tracks, astonished. Totò had been so difficult for so long . . . but the sight of him bounding forward, like when he was a little boy and wanted to be caught and swung round by his dad . . .

Smiling, he almost held out his arms in response. His son bounded straight past without seeing him. The marshal turned with a puzzled frown and saw Totò with his hands on the shoulders of a slim, fair girl. He was talking earnestly. She was listening with her head down, a head of long, loose curls that reached to her waist, like a Botticelli painting. Her arms were held stiffly by her sides, her fingers gripping the overlong sleeves of a dark T-shirt. The marshal turned away and walked home alone.

*   *   *

In the afternoon the waiting room was full, but a glance around the worried or hopeful faces told him there was nothing Lorenzini couldn't deal with. He walked through with a polite greeting and shut himself in his office with the stuff from the Japanese girl's flat.

As he sat down and drew the pile on the desk towards him, he was still thinking about Totò. He'd never been an easy child, not

137

compared with Giovanni. It was impossible not to admire his intelligence and quickness, though. And now . . . you had to hand it to him, vegetarian or not, that was a lovely girl. His place at table had been empty again but Teresa hadn't even had to look at him. He kept quiet.

It had been Giovanni who'd told them that the girl's parents were separating and that, as soon as term ended, she was to move back to Denmark with her mother:

—He says he's going to run away. He won't, though, will he, Mum?

—Of course he won't. And give me that T-shirt after. You've splashed tomato on it and I've still to do a dark wash. Does anybody want any more?

You thought your children were children for ever and then, all of a sudden, they weren't. A lovely girl, but foreign. The Japanese girl had run away from her family and look how that had ended up.

His respect for his younger son was redoubled but he felt worried.

Small children, small problems, they say.

And if they suddenly stopped being children, the world looked completely different.

His son had run straight past, not even seeing him, and now he felt as lonely as if they'd both left home. After all, one day they would.

138

Just get on with your work, he told himself, opening the folder in front of him. No danger of that running away.

Of course, he'd have to retire when the moment came . . .

Everything in your life that seems so solid and permanent is really shifting underneath you without your noticing.

Lorenzini's head appearing round the door was a welcome sight. 'Visitor for you.'

It was Beppe, the oldest gardener, his face bursting with self-importance, peering through the fronds of a huge plant.

'Come in, come in . . . what on earth have you got there?'

'A *Kentia*. It won't dirty your floor, there's a plastic dish under it. We've had a delivery and I thought this would do nicely in here. I'll put it near the window. It's to say thank you.'

'Thank you?'

'You remember? That flat you suggested for my granddaughter? They're moving in on the first of next month. Don't overwater it. Now: what I've really come about is that shoe. You'd better come with me—we've not touched it. I said right away to Giovanni, I said, they'll be wanting to take photographs like they did up at the pool. Am I right?'

'I—quite right, yes. Where did you—'

'Shall we go, then?'

As they started up the gravel path Beppe, despite his age, his girth and the steepness of the climb, chattered on, breathless.' It was because of last night's storm, you see. We always have to check all the drains after a storm. It was one of those, look. D'you see?'

The pale gravel, only superficially dry as yet, was interrupted every few metres by a diagonal stone runnel leading to what looked like a tiny sepulchre at the side.

'We have to go left here and go up the main avenue a bit.'

The main avenue was even steeper and Beppe fell silent for a while, catching his breath.

'How much further up?' the marshal asked.

'Not far now. Where Giovanni's standing guard. We thought he should stay there, just in case . . .'

The broad stretch of sand-coloured gravel rose to a glistening horizon crowned by the silhouette of a stone staircase and an equestrian statue. Huge fluffy white clouds drifted above in the deep-blue sky and everything smelled of wet laurel leaves.

Giovanni, the head gardener, stood back when they reached him so that the marshal could take a look. 'We haven't touched it. I suppose you'll take photographs like you did up at the pool. You're lucky. These drains may not be much bigger than your hand, but once you're behind the opening they're enormous. If it had been pushed harder it'd have gone down and you'd never have seen it again.

Stuck like that with the heel caught, a fair bit of gravel and some leaves and stuff washed up against it during the storm so it wasn't draining properly and we spotted it.'

'I knew right away it was the one you were looking for,' said Beppe, 'and it is, isn't it?'

'Yes, it is.' The marshal straightened up and looked about him. 'The pool where we found her must be up there to the right. If our man went straight down this avenue, he didn't take the nearest exit, the Annalena one . . .'

Below them, at the foot of the main avenue, lay the biggest pool with its central island, the Porta Romana exit and the ring roads. That was the exit furthest from Peruzzi's workshop, from Peruzzi himself, from Issino, from the Japanese girl's flat, from her world. People who came into the city by car parked outside the city walls near the Porta Romana. The boyfriend, maybe . . . Rome. Who'd mentioned Rome? Lapo . . . or Peruzzi? Peruzzi, slamming the door, purple with anger, shouting:

—If she's not in Rome, I don't know where she is!

But Lapo had said something about a friend in Rome. Was all that anger really about loutish tourists or were they just a cover for Peruzzi's jealousy?

—If you've got time to be running after young people who don't know their own minds . . .

141

Anxious to get back to his office and those letters and photographs, he left as soon as the technician arrived on the scene. As his feet crunched downhill, he could hear Beppe, his breath quite recovered, elaborating on his story as he told it again.

'The marshal knows my name and address if you need to get in touch with me.'

'I don't think I'll need to do that—stand out of the way, will you . . .'

He quickened his pace. Back at the station he found the waiting room empty. He looked in at the door of the duty room where he could hear the crackle of the motorbike patrol calling in.

'Everything all right?'

The young carabiniere at the console looked up. 'Fine. All quiet.'

'Lorenzini?'

'He's got somebody with him. A woman. She was crying her eyes out. I could hear her from in here but she seems to have quietened down now.'

'Oh, Lord, I bet it's Monica . . . Listen, when he's finished, tell him I'm in my office and I don't want to be disturbed for an hour at least—and don't put any calls through.'

'All right.'

But when a weeping Monica had been shown out, the bike patrol had come in and a good two hours had gone by, he was still sitting at his desk, too shocked to speak. When

142

Lorenzini at last opened the door, looking puzzled, the marshal could find no words and only stared at him, unseeing.

'What's the matter with you? What's happened?'

The marshal dropped his head into his hands and rubbed hard at his eyes. Then, with a deep breath, he pulled himself together. 'You'd better come in.'

CHAPTER SEVEN

'Have you rung Borgognissanti?'

'No.'

'You haven't talked to anybody?'

'No.' How could he explain? He'd been sitting there for goodness knows how long like somebody paralysed because once he moved, once he acted on what he'd seen, told somebody, it would become real. He'd been practically holding his breath, trying to stop the world turning. It was his responsibility, no getting away from that. His fault. And now there was Lorenzini drumming his fingers, his body tense with impatience.

'I was thinking . . .' he lied, 'I don't want to make things worse . . .'

'How much worse can it get? She's dead. What's worse than dead?' Lorenzini looked at him the way he always did when his aggressive good sense came up against what he referred to as Sicilianity. He had learned over the years to be patient but you could see he felt this was no time for treading tactfully around what he saw as his superior's slow southern ways.

'Do you want me to call? Or go over there? What's the problem? We've got to move!' He didn't even try to keep the irritation out of his voice. 'Can you imagine what will happen if the newspapers get to this first?'

'Yes.'

Lapo had said it: 'Good God, if I'd told what I know it'd be on the front page . . .

The photographs lay spread all over the desk between them. Views of red roofs, domes and towers from Piazzale Michelangelo, views of the Arno valley from Bellosguardo, the Ponte Vecchio from the Santa Trinita Bridge, Peruzzi and Issino in their long aprons at the door of the workshop, close-ups of shoes, details of shoes, skeletons of shoes.

And then a whole packet of pictures of him. Eyes alight, handsome face a little flushed, the same face as Totò when he'd bounded past his father today, the face of someone in love.

'Telephone him.'

'What?'

'Or, better still, send somebody round there and have him brought in. There's no time to waste! He could disappear if this gets out!'

'He already has.' The marshal watched Lorenzini's face. He'd known him so long. The more aggressive he seemed, the more upset he was. He was very upset now. 'You're right, of course, about the papers. It'll be a scandal anyway, but as far as disappearing's concerned, it's too late. I said I haven't told anybody and I haven't, but since Captain Maestrangelo had asked me particularly to keep an eye, I felt I could call the signora without any sort of explanation and I did. It was a shock when she answered so . . . cheerfully. She seemed really pleased to hear from me but, of course, she realised right away that I wouldn't call for no reason.'

—Has something happened to him?

—No, no, Signora . . .

—It's such a dangerous job. I can't help worrying.

—Nothing like that, I promise you. I just wanted to check something with him . . . a case we've been working on. How are you, anyway? I was sorry to hear about your illness.

'She laughed and said she'd never been ill in her life. I got round that by saying I must have been mistaken, just an impression. I said her son probably worried about her falling ill, given that she was alone, the way she worried about something happening to him because he did a dangerous job. She didn't pick it up, just said she missed him and was looking forward to his next leave.'

'He didn't go home.'

'No. She hasn't seen him since Easter when he brought his girlfriend home. She had a lot to say about that, said she was a lovely girl but—'

'Foreign.'

'Yes. They all did their best. It's a big family and they all invited her. Not a day went by without there being a family dinner at one aunt's or another's but despite all the hospitality there'd been a quarrel of some sort. She said she wasn't the interfering kind but

146

marriage is difficult enough without the problems two different cultures are likely to cause. He seemed so head over heels in love, though, that her only hope was that it would wear off. She hoped I'd back her up if . . . if he confided in me.'

Lorenzini dropped into the chair in front of the marshal's desk. His aggressiveness had dissipated as the full implications sank in. It was the man's disappearance that made the case as bad as it could get. So he, too, fell as silent as the marshal for a moment. Twenty-six colour photographs of Esposito lay spread on the desk between them, handsome, happy and glowing with love.

'Oh, for Christ's sake . . .' was all Lorenzini could manage at last. 'Oh, for Christ's sake!'

*   *   *

It rained again during the night, steady, heavy rain with distant grumblings of thunder. The marshal lay in the dark, his eyes wide open. Every so often a faint wash of light managed to get between the slats of the closed outer shutters and for a second he saw a paler darkness of long muslin curtain, then it all went black. Heavier curtains would shut the storm out. Or solid inside shutters. Each spent flash provoked an answering flicker of irritation. For God's sake, how was he supposed to sleep? He hadn't got to bed until

147

one in the morning and tomorrow promised to be a long and heavy day. Teresa had only given him a bowl of the light broth she'd prepared for tomorrow with some bread in it and a sprinkling of cheese.

—You know you always have nightmares if you eat late at night.

Well, there was little enough danger of having any nightmares tonight, with the room lighting up like a firework display every few minutes, and on top of that he was starving. The stormy air was sticky and his thin cotton pyjamas felt like they were made of serge. Either they or the sheets were damp and creased under his back. He tried wriggling his shoulders to smooth things out but only managed to make more creases. He turned on his side and pushed the top sheet down. Four o'clock. It would be easier to sleep with the bedside light on than with this blasted flashing but he didn't want to wake Teresa. Installing inside shutters would be an expense but surely a bit of a curtain wasn't too much to ask! What was she thinking about? That thin stuff wouldn't keep anything out. If you couldn't be safe in your own house, where could you be safe?

Should he get up and check on the boys again? She'd be annoyed if she woke up and noticed. She'd been annoyed when he went in before:

—It's after midnight. You'll wake them up.

—I won't.

—Well, don't switch the light on. You know how you used to wake them up when they were small.

—I never saw them when they were small. I was here on my own, wasn't I? I missed their whole childhood!

—Don't exaggerate, Salva. And don't wake them up.

So he hadn't switched the light on, just stood there in the doorway, listening to their breathing. He'd even resisted the temptation to cover Totò with his tumbled sheets since it was so hot anyway.

You thought you could help them, protect them, but then it turned out that you couldn't do a thing. They weren't your children, they were just other people. You might as well not be there. It seemed as if every time that faint flash of light came it was a signal for the scene to play over again in his head. Totò bounding towards him, calling *Where were you?* Each time it played he wanted to open his arms and swing his laughing little boy round and round. But each time, Totò bounded past without seeing him.

So he wouldn't get up. He'd only disturb them. Teresa was right.

—Don't say anything to him. Promise me.

With the next flash came the thought of Esposito, the one thought he really must keep out if he wanted any sleep at all. His first name was Lorenzo. His mother, on the phone, had called him Enzo. She was a widow but she sounded young, cheerful. Women got on all right without men around, getting in their way. But he couldn't get along without Teresa . . .

He'd lied about his mother being ill. That was going to go against him. There might or might not be evidence of him in her flat but DNA would prove if the child was his. There were the photographs and there were witnesses. That restaurant was packed last night, full of Japanese fashion people here for the menswear show. The owner had recognised Esposito from the photographs right away. Tomorrow he was going to have to go back to Peruzzi, Lapo, all of them.

It was only natural that they'd all thought he was accusing Peruzzi to protect Esposito. We all protect our own, as Lapo said. Up to that point they'd been so helpful, so discreet, avoiding mentioning Esposito, trusting him. Lapo saying nothing more than: —What a nasty mess, especially for you . . . but I know you'll do your duty—Peruzzi, distressed as he was, swearing he wouldn't talk to journalists. They'd been trying to help him and he hadn't understood. He'd spent a long time closeted with Lorenzini, going over first, the timetable of events, as well as could be managed without a precise time of death, then the information he had failed to pick up on in the little square. Stuff that had been meaningless at the time.

150

Peruzzi saying:

—How can you be sure . . . but of course you'd know. And then:

—I could have sworn she was in love . . . She was in love . . . the baby would have kept her.

—I could have done a lot for them. We had plans. Did he tell you?

Well, no, he didn't tell me because . . . He bundled himself back into the damp, creasy sheets but they were intolerable and he got up again. Because he didn't feel he could confide in me. Because I don't understand anything and my own wife is keeping me away from my son because I'd only upset him. If she'd been able to keep me away from Esposito we might not be in this mess. No. That was rubbish because, by that time the Japanese girl was dead. Before then, Esposito had been doing well.

Lorenzini had talked to the men, not telling them why, asking them if they knew anything about Esposito's girlfriend, especially Di Nuccio who was from Naples and had been the one to say Esposito must be in love. But all he knew was that Esposito used to go out fairly often, all spruced up, and then he stopped. He'd just assumed. Of course he hadn't confided in any of them. He was an NCO and a newly made one at that, hardly likely to get pally with the men. Lorenzini himself was his immediate superior. Esposito was living in barracks, far from home and old friends.

151

There was nobody. There should have been the marshal. The young man was under his care and if he had felt unable to confide in him, that was the marshal's failure.

'I'll make you some camomile tea.' The light went on.

'What?'

'Salva, you've been trailing around the room in the dark for the last half-hour and the sheets on your side look like a battleground. Make the bed and I'll bring us some camomile. D'you want a bit of honey in it?'

'Yes, and . . .'

'And what?'

'Are there any biscuits?'

*   *   *

In the morning it was still pouring down. The marshal had himself driven the short distance to the little square. The rain-sodden flags hung limp and dirtied. There were few people about. If he was going to have to spend his morning apologising for himself, he'd start with Santini, the restorer, and work his way up. By the time he got to Peruzzi he'd be better informed, better prepared. There was a spotlight glowing in Santini's window, illuminating a painted kitchen cupboard and a well bucket full of fresh flowers, but nobody appeared when the marshal went in and the bell rang.

152

'Anybody there?'

The first room was as dark as the day. A dozen large decorated bowls stood on a long table and there was a small desk which the marshal looked at as he waited. It must have been very old because there was a worn patch in the middle at the front and a burned-in depression on the right hand edge. Somebody had spent a good many hours with his feet up, smoking a cigar. A man at peace with himself and the world.

The marshal sighed and called out again, 'Anybody there?'

He knew there must be because he could hear violin music and work going on, sandpapering, he thought, somewhere behind.

'Come back later. I'm busy!'

The marshal edged his way down a corridor stacked with picture frames and half blocked by a marble sink leaning against the wall. 'Santini!'

The young restorer appeared at the end of the corridor in a rectangle of light. His old clothes were spattered with paint and varnish, his long curly hair tied back with a rag. 'Oh, it's you . . .'

He turned back to the cupboard door he was working on, sandpapering away dark-green paint from its edges to show brown wood. He acknowledged the marshal's presence beside him by reaching to turn off the radio. 'What can I do for you?' The tone

153

suggested that, whatever it was, he wasn't going to do it.

The marshal followed the rhythmic movement of his hand a while, thinking. Then he laid his cards on the table. 'Listen, Santini, I didn't know.'

'Eh?'

'About Esposito.'

'Oh . . . that was his name, was it . . .'

'Do you believe me or not?'

Santini put down the sandpaper on a cluttered workbench and took up a rag that smelled of turps. He began rubbing in silence.

'So?' The marshal stood his ground, insisting.

After a long wait, Santini at last threw down the rag and looked him in the face. 'Yes. I believe you. You're probably the only southerner on the face of the earth I would believe and I don't know why I do but . . . If you want to know, none of us knew anything either, until she'd gone. He didn't hang out around here and Akiko was very close about her private life. But then Peruzzi got so agitated and started talking. There'd been a row that had really upset her and Peruzzi blamed him.'

'What was the row about. Do you know?'

He took up the rag and went back to his rubbing. 'All I know is what Peruzzi told me. Your man wanted to marry her and she wouldn't, not even when she was pregnant.'

'Did you know her well?'

'She was one of us, a real craftsman. That's all.' He took a soft dry cloth and rubbed with gentle strokes so different from his harsh voice.

'It's just that everybody who's talked about her said she was so precise, organised, determined, too. What I mean is, these days, if a woman doesn't want children . . .'

Santini snorted. 'What people think they want and what they really need don't necessarily coincide, do they? That's when "accidentally on purpose" kicks in. Natural forces care nothing for our half-baked ideas of how our lives should go. Life is what happens to us while we're making other plans, right?' He rubbed harder, then bundled the cloth up and threw it down on the bench.

'You sound as if you learned that lesson the hard way.'

'Is there another way to learn it?'

The smell of turps was very strong. The marshal took a step back, waiting in silence.

Santini dribbled thin, pale-green paint down the door, disturbed its meandering progress with the soaked rag, stood back to look. 'Your next question is "Are you married yourself?" No, I'm not. And no, I'm not gay. I have the occasional fling but . . . look around you. I rent two small rooms on the first floor and they don't look all that different from this one. This is how I live, who I am. What sort of woman

155

would marry me?'

The marshal thought, a woman like Akiko. He didn't say it. He couldn't afford to put his foot in it again. Best put that one on the back burner until he'd done the rounds, heard everybody.

Santini worked on in concentrated silence for some time. Then he looked at the marshal, ironic, almost smiling. 'You're thinking Akiko. I wish . . . No, that won't take you anywhere, but thanks for the compliment. I could never have moved her in that way. Your man must have had something special.'

'Did you meet him?'

'No. Never saw him until he showed up that day in uniform and then it was only a glimpse. Good-looking. But that's not what counts, is it? There are some men who can impregnate a woman just by looking at her. D'you know what I mean? Perhaps he's one of them. What do you think? You should know.'

He should know, but he didn't. Behind Santini, a metal door stood open on a gloomy little courtyard, no more than a well in the building, where stone and marble sinks leaned against the dirty walls and old paint tins and buckets were clustered in the middle. The rain came on heavier, clattering, splashing and drumming on everything in its way. It was growing darker.

*   *   *

Swish and clack, swish and clack, the printing press drowned out the noise of the rain. The fruity smell of ink filled the little front room where a young assistant was packing wedding invitations into white boxes.

'He's gone to the bank. He reckons it's less crowded than Fridays but he'll be hours, even so.'

'He doesn't send you? It can't be much fun, at his age, standing for hours in a queue.'

'No chance of him sending me. Nobody touches his money. Besides, it's a gossip shop. And he's usually had a coffee and a grappa when he gets back.' His glance strayed to the open newspaper on a stool at his side, open at the football page. While the cat's away . . . he would no doubt go back to it when the marshal left.

'I suppose you know about Peruzzi's Japanese girl?' The marshal, too, shot a glance at the paper but there would be nothing in there until after tomorrow morning's news conference.

'Everybody's talking about it and about . . .' He tailed off, shooting a glance at the gold flame on the soaked hat the marshal was holding.

'About her carabiniere boyfriend?'

'They say Peruzzi hasn't heard from him for ages and that—'

'That what? That maybe he killed her, is

that what they're saying?'

'No! Nobody . . . that you're keeping him away. You know . . . to avoid a scandal. That's all. I didn't mean . . He was blushing and he swallowed hard, his Adam's apple prominent in his thin neck. He was very young, still had a trace of acne.

'That's all right. It's only natural they should talk about it.' The last thing he wanted was to frighten the lad. He needed all the friends he could get in the square now. Remembering the oldest gardener's complaint, he was glad that he wasn't wearing his black glasses. He hated the rain like a cat hates the rain but at least, in this weather, he could see without the streaming tears that sunshine provoked.

'Anyway, you can tell him when he comes back that we're not keeping this a secret, we just didn't know about it until now and, you'll see, it'll be in the paper the day after tomorrow So if he knows anything he should get in touch with me. All right?' The young man's face showed that it wasn't all right, that the dead weight of anxiety that was hurting the marshal's chest was communicating itself. The young man stared at him, uncertain how to answer. Say something casual . . .

'Well, I'll let you get back to your football. Pleased they're back in the first division?'

'If they stay there this time.'

'They'll stay there. It just needed Della Valle's money. That's what counts these days

158

. . .' That was the best he could do but he could hear the false note in his own voice.

Swish and clack and out through the frosted-glass door into the rain. Adjusting his hat and turning up the collar of his black rainproof, he splashed through a puddle in the uneven paving to the huge open doors of the packing warehouse, knowing it was likely to be the same story there. Nevertheless, he called out and waited among mummified statues and bundled chandeliers in the high room until an old man appeared to tell him that the packer, too, had gone to the bank. He explained his errand and left. The printer and the packer were much of an age and were, no doubt, in the bar having a grappa by now. Santini, the restorer, was another generation. Lapo fell somewhere in between but it wasn't difficult to guess where he would attach himself.

It was his plump daughter, stacking plates in the half-lit back room, who told him. 'Dad's gone to the bank. If you want to come back later, it's stuffed pork roll today . . .'

In the warm light of the kitchen behind her mother was bent over the open oven door, basting the pork. Granny was parked in the corner behind her where she spent all her days since a tiny stroke had frightened her. She was peeling potatoes in the lap of her apron and dropping them in a bucket at her feet. Even at this early hour, the smell of the roast scented with rosemary provoked a sharp twinge of hunger.

'No, no . . . Just ask him to call me this afternoon, and tell him . . .'

Pausing on the doorstep, looking out at the dark rain splattering on to bare plastic tables, he had to admit to himself that he was relieved to have had this opportunity of 'throwing his hat in first'. Now, when he did talk to them, the air should have cleared.

As for being prepared for Peruzzi, how do you prepare yourself for a minefield? You tread carefully, that's all. What did it matter anyway, now? To think that, only the other day, he'd been sitting here in the sunshine with a glass of wine in front of him and nothing more on his mind than a regular murder case involving a foreigner. No political or powerful connections, no distressed parents, no press harassment, no pressure from the prosecutor's office, his only problem a bad-tempered shoemaker.

Hunching his shoulders against the heavy rods of rain, he made for the workshop. Thunder cracked above his bowed head, preparing him for Peruzzi's flashing anger.

*   *   *

Akiko's death had hit Peruzzi hard. His sharp gaze seemed without direction, as if he were wandering in a maze. The marshal himself had been obliged to wander through a maze to get

160

to him because he wasn't in the workshop. Surely, after all the grand talk about his son's seeing to everything, he hadn't gone to the bank with the others? Just for the chat and the visit to the bar? No, Issino had told him.

—In shop. Signora goes for coffee. This way please.

And instead of having to go out into the storm, walk some way down the street and turn back into Borgo San Jacopo, he had been sent down an ill-lit staircase and instructed to go left, right, right, along to the end, round behind cupboards, open door on right and up the stairs. The subterranean corridor was better lit than the stairs and if things had been as they should be, he'd have been interested by the shelves along each side with their boxes and lasts and stacks of new leather. But things were not as they should be and he went along with hardly a turn of the head to where, after a mistake that revealed to him Issino's cubbyhole room and another ending in a store cupboard, he had hit the right door and come up to the surface.

The woman who looked after the shop had already come back from her break, cutting it short, perhaps, to dodge the worsening storm. He'd found her kneeling amid a scatter of shoes at the feet of a customer, making soothing noises. Peruzzi had been standing with a stack of boxes in his arms, looking out at the rain, so he hadn't noticed the marshal's

161

arrival until he'd gone forward and touched his elbow. 'We have to talk.'

Peruzzi had turned that distracted gaze to him then, but after five or six minutes, when he'd made a few sharp comments and the customer had left without buying anything, the shop assistant had suggested they sit down or perhaps go back to the workshop. The marshal still hadn't got his attention.

Peruzzi, even more than the marshal, looked so out of place in the elegant, blue-carpeted shop, too big and lanky with his long apron and his workman's hands. This other world was all soft lights and pale colours, and smelled faintly of perfume as well as new shoes.

'The signora's right, Peruzzi. Let's go back to the workshop.'

But he got no answer and a blonde young woman came into the shop to interrupt them. She was smiling, holding a dripping umbrella. The assistant hurried forward to take it but the blond customer was looking at Peruzzi.

'Your apprentice sent me round. Have you made those moccasins?'

'Yes, I have. Light-brown or dark.'

'But I wanted a red pair and a blue pair like last year! Don't you remember? I came in at the end of April and you said they'd be ready at the beginning of June.'

'Well, they are ready. They're in the window, aren't they?'

162

'But they're brown!'

'I've only made brown this year. You don't want moccasins in fancy colours.'

'But, Peruzzi, you made them last year!'

'Well, I'm not making them this year.'

'You promised me. You said June.' She looked for help to the shop woman who murmured, 'I'll talk to him. Come back next week.' She signed to the marshal to get Peruzzi back to the workshop where he belonged.

Inspired by the thought of the shelves down below, he suggested, 'Let me help you take all these boxes of shoes back down. I don't suppose you want them cluttering up the shop.'

'It's not the shoes that clutter up this shop.' No doubt the customers did. Still, at least they got going and the marshal followed him down, helping him with the boxes to be stacked on the shelves of the long corridor. The only way to engage Peruzzi's attention in his present distracted state was through shoes. From that he could move easily enough to Akiko, then to Esposito and the quarrel.

'Not there.' Peruzzi took the boxes from him. 'I've got this new system. Where there's a size missing I leave a gap. That way . . . It was Akiko's idea.' He stopped, losing the thread of what he was saying, of what he was doing.

'You miss her a lot.'

'We had plans, you see. I offered to help them buy a house, did he tell you that?'

'Peruzzi, I didn't know about Esposito. I had no idea. He's been with us seven or eight months but it's not as though I was in his confidence. I wish I had been, I feel now I should have been, but there it is. And now he's gone and I need your help.'

'No. If you're trying to accuse him of what happened to Akiko, no.'

'I'm not accusing anybody, I'm trying to find out what happened.'

'It could have been anybody. In a public park it could have been anybody at all. Some drug addict, somebody trying to steal something—and what if it was an accident!'

'Don't get agitated. Remember your heart— if it was an accident we have to establish that. We have to talk to Esposito and we don't know where he is.'

'He loved her. She was having his child and he wanted to marry her.'

'But she wouldn't marry him, would she? They quarrelled, you know they did. Why are you defending him? Santini said you blamed him. You told me yourself she was crying as she worked.'

'She loved him.'

'So why wouldn't she marry him?'

'Because she'd just got free! You don't know what it cost her. The worst thing was leaving her sister but she gave up everything, money, security, her own country, everything for the freedom to live the way she wanted, think the

164

way she wanted.'

'And didn't she want Esposito? If she loved him, like you say?'

'She did love him. She would have married him, she told me that. But then they went down to Naples and she found out that she wouldn't be marrying Enzo, she'd be marrying his entire family. She said she'd escaped from one cage and flown halfway round the world and into another. They don't understand when they're young that life gets hard. You need your family. I don't know how I'd have managed on my own when my wife died. I'd have let things go. If it hadn't been for my son I think I'd have gone, too. I had this heart trouble, even then. Life plays nasty tricks on you—I mean—who'd have thought little Akiko would go before me? We had such plans . . .'

The marshal placed a hand on his angular shoulder. 'Think about your health, Peruzzi. As long as you've got that, there'll be other plans. You thought you couldn't go on when your wife died. But you did go on. And Akiko, you didn't know that Akiko would come along but she did come along, out of nowhere. So you just concentrate on keeping well and let me worry about Esposito. Let's go up to the workshop and when we get there you can tell me about any other friends or acquaintance Akiko might have had, especially anyone outside Florence who might have come to see her that day. You mentioned a friend in Rome the other day, and Lapo said he'd heard that from you, too. Was it a man or a woman?'

'A man. Somebody she knew when she was studying art history. I don't know his name or anything.'

'But they were still in touch?'

'Yes, they kept in touch. She went down there not long ago.'

'Then I'll find him in her address book. You see I'm not just accusing Esposito—though—'

'I only met him that once but I can tell you, he loved her. He wanted the child. He'd have looked after her.'

'We have to find him, then we'll see. This friend in Rome, too. Who's to say it wasn't him?'

'Or an accident, like I said.'

The marshal didn't want to say too much, at least for the moment, but he had to take that hope away.

'I don't think so, Peruzzi. You see, we found her other shoe.'

When they parted company, the last thing Peruzzi said was, 'When this is all over, I don't suppose . . . I'd like to have those shoes—I'm not the sentimental sort, don't think that. I just thought Issino might like them. Yes. You see— well, he could learn a lot, I mean, she'd not been here a year when she made them. It's not that I—'

'No. No, of course not. It might be some time but I'll bring them to you myself.'

166

His carabiniere driver had already started the engine. Blue exhaust smoke hung low in the rain. As he got into the car, wetting everything he touched, the radio coughed into life.

'Marshal? Can you go straight to headquarters?'

'What's happened?'

'They wouldn't say. Just that you should go there and that it's urgent.'

'Is Lorenzini there?'

'He's in your office.'

'Tell him to call me on my mobile.'

When it rang, he kept his face averted and his voice low. 'What's happened?'

'They've found him.'

'Where?'

'Rome. You're going to have to go down there. They'll tell you the details at headquarters but I'd better warn you: it's not good.'

CHAPTER EIGHT

He was tired. So tired that in spite of the steepness of the climb he could feel his eyes closing and his heavy head dropping, even as he plodded upwards. He tried to prop his head against the rough wing of his seat but he couldn't help his mouth hanging open. He hoped he wasn't snoring. He did snore in trains, Teresa said. He shifted his shoulder a bit until he felt his head securely lodged, then went on with his exhausting climb up the gravel path. Beppe, the gardener, was still beside him but they were never going to catch up with the Japanese girl at this rate. She was much higher up and trotting faster than ever. In any case, it was so dark he could hardly make her out at all.

—You want to take those sunglasses off.

That was the gardener's voice, though he couldn't see him properly either. He tried taking off his dark glasses but it made no difference at all and the effort of trying to see in the gloom tired him even more.

—How much further is it?

Beppe didn't answer. If it wasn't his dark glasses that prevented him from seeing, what was it? The main lights in the carriage were off because everybody was sleeping but that wouldn't account for it because it couldn't be night-time in the Boboli Gardens. They close at sunset.

*　　　*　　　*

'Sandwiches, coffee, mineral water, soft drinks!'

That was in the train. They don't sell stuff like that in the gardens. The gardener said:

—This is a dream . . .

—I know that. I know, but I don't want to go up there alone.

Where was the Japanese girl? And how could she run on this gravel without her shoes?

He didn't ask the question aloud but the gardener answered anyway:

—She's still wearing them.

—She can't be wearing them. We've got them. She's dead.

—She won't be dead until she gets to the pool. That's why I'm carrying this plant.

That explained why he couldn't see the gardener. The plant was so big he was hidden behind it. They climbed for a while in silence and then the gardener said:

—The plant in her apartment's dead. You didn't water it.

—I couldn't . . . I had to do so many other things.

—Other things can wait. If you don't water a plant it dies. It can't wait.

—But it was too late! It was already dead. I

169

didn't know about the girl. I didn't know about Esposito. Why does nobody believe me?

—They do believe you. That's why they're all waiting for you. We have to turn right here.

Laurel leaves brushed against his right cheek, scratching him, but he kept it pressed against the seat wing, anyway, to stop his heading falling. They turned left and started climbing again and it seemed to be getting a bit lighter. When the marshal realised why, his heart began thumping hard and beads of sweat formed at his temples. He kept his eyes lowered, fixed on the gravel which was sliding below his feet like a river. It would have been impossible to turn back without losing his balance and besides, he realised now, people were coming up behind him and they were closing in, chattering, bustling, pushing. They must be journalists, people from the prosecutor's office, the people from the train . . .

The light coming from the top of the path intensified, flashing, flashing, sending shockwaves through him. He pushed his head lower and squeezed his eyes shut but nothing would keep the light out and nothing could stop his inexorable upward slide towards the pool.

He was suffocating and his neck hurt. Despite his efforts to block his head against the seat wing, it dropped down so that his chin pressed against his chest, blocking his windpipe. He couldn't fight his way to the surface of consciousness enough to readjust it. He knew he must be snoring now and, what was worse, he couldn't control the trickle of saliva he could feel was forming in the right corner of his mouth.

'He must be exhausted . . .'

'Can you manage?'

'I think so . . . thank you. Excuse me.'

Comforting voices. If he'd been able to, he'd have moved his left leg to help them but he couldn't. He wanted them to keep talking, to keep him in the cosy darkened world of the train but they fell silent and the background noise of the train itself wasn't enough to hold him. It was fading and the world was getting lighter, flashing, flashing . . .

—You can see her now if you look up.

He didn't want to but he had to. He had to lift his head, the gardener was right. He'd stopped breathing. With a choking snort he moved and his head swung away from safety, out into the void where the light was so bright. He was looking up the steep gravel path to the horizon but it wasn't true that he could see her. All he saw against the glaring sky was an equestrian statue. It was the one that was always there, the gardener ought to know that, since he worked here.

—That's her. Never walks if she can trot.

But when they reached the botanical garden there was no sign of the equestrian statue.

171

The gate was padlocked. They had to clamber over barbed wire and push through a high laurel hedge. He saw her standing with her back to him at the edge of the pool, looking down into it. She wasn't as small as he'd thought. She was still wearing her shoes, so perhaps he could get to her in time, but he was walking so slowly, his legs as heavy as lead. He daren't call to her, afraid she would trot away from him. He was getting a little bit closer. But shouldn't her hair have been black? Or was he remembering the black hairy roots of the water hyacinth around her? No. She was Japanese. No Japanese ever had that long fair hair, curling down to the waist. How could he have got everything so wrong? Why couldn't he even remember her name?

She and the pool were drifting away from him.

—Wait! I'm sorry! I just didn't recognise you!

—I know.

Her voice was far away, cold and very sad.

—It's because I have no face.

Further and further away.

—Wait! Please wait! Akiko! Your name is Akiko!

But it was too late.

The gardener said: —She's dead now. Look in the pool.

He didn't want to look but they were all standing there waiting, Peruzzi, Lapo, Santini, everyone.

So he stepped forward into the bright light, his heart thumping, sweat rolling down his temples. He'd thought he was on the train already, but when he reached the edge of the pool they made him step up on the ledge and walk along it, trying to keep his balance, until they reached almost the end of the platform. Then they all climbed into the train and pushed along the centre aisle. The railway police were there as well as the carabinieri and a magistrate. They all stood back to let him through and somebody said:

—It's his father.

He stopped at the edge of the pool of thickened blood. The door of the lavatory had been broken down and stood leaning to one side. Esposito was hunkered down in the tiny space but his head was raised, leaning against the wall. His handsome face, seen in profile, was perfect. He was smiling. The marshal's heart lifted. It wasn't too late!

—Listen, Esposito, it's going to be all right. I promise you. I'll help you. We'll all help you.

He talked to Esposito for a long time. He got no answer but it didn't matter. What mattered was that, as he talked, the light felt warm and pleasant on his face and his breathing grew more gentle. Esposito understood the words which the marshal himself couldn't hear all that clearly except in snatches.

—And on your birthday we'll go to Lapo's place for a good meal and everybody who cares for you will be there.

—You can eat whatever you want, it doesn't matter.

—You'll be happy, you'll see. We want you to eat. You must eat to stay alive, that's all we want.

—Do you understand?

He understood. His handsome face, still in profile, still smiling . . .

—And look, just look how the sunshine warms your glass of wine and makes that red spot on the white—no, don't touch it. Don't turn round.

They were surrounded by such a warm glow that everything must be all right now.

—We won't tell your mother, that will be best. We won't tell her.

—Everything will be all right. You'll get better with time.

The chattering voices were quiet. Nobody disturbed them.

There was no hurry, after all, to get back to his office so they walked through the gardens. Lorenzini would be looking after things. What was there to worry about? Esposito had been upset and needed a rest. That's all there was to it. They must take it gently. So they walked together and the marshal talked to him, encouraging him, keeping him going. It didn't matter that he couldn't hear his own words

174

and Esposito couldn't hear them either. It only mattered that there was a voice, very close by, soothing.

It wasn't dark any more. He could see every pebble, every leaf. A double row of potted lemon trees crossed the great pool towards Poseidon on his island. The scene was so brightly lit that the lemons glittered and orange flickers appeared and disappeared in the green water.

—No. Throw the bread but don't touch the water.

—Look at that massive one! That could eat you!

—It couldn't, could it, Dad?

—No. They're only teasing you. Come away.

Esposito came away without protest but he seemed very quiet.

—We can sit down if you're tired. This stone seat's nice and smooth.

But they didn't stop. The sun warmed the side of the marshal's forehead and it felt pleasant but what about Esposito? The handsome profile was still smiling but the other side?

—It's better now—Esposito said.

They were turning right and climbing.

—No . . . don't go up there. You mustn't go up there.

Esposito didn't listen. The marshal felt him growing colder and sadder.

—Wait . . . Let's go back.

175

But he knew they couldn't. They climbed on until they reached the botanical garden and Esposito went in to where the crowd was waiting.

—No . . .

Esposito was laying himself down in the shallow pool. Forli's voice described in detail what was happening, though he wasn't there. The marshal understood that the voice must be coming from a tape recorder somewhere and he was content because Forli understood the dead.

—It'll only take one drop of water, you'll see.

Esposito pushed the barrel up his nose. It looked like a water pistol but it was really his Beretta 9. One side of his face remained perfect, a friendly dark eye watching the marshal. But then the face cracked open right down the centre and the other side split away to glare in the opposite direction at the crowd, a creased half-mask, leaving a white and bloody mess in between. The photographers moved in with flash after flash after flash after flash after flash . . .

*   *   *

'Tickets, please.'

The marshal jerked awake. The sun was coming up and warming his brow through the glass. Telegraph poles rushed by the window

176

making the low light blink and blink and blink. The open fields beyond were still pearly white. His eyes were watering.

'Your ticket, please?'

Still trapped inside his dream, mouth dry, head pounding, he struggled to find his ticket and handed it over.

'Have a pleasant journey. Good morning.' The inspector withdrew.

The woman in the opposite window seat looked at the marshal with sympathy. 'You were so tired. It's a shame he woke you.'

'I'm sorry. I must have been snoring.'

'Don't worry. Everybody else was asleep and I don't mind.' She kept her voice low since the other passengers were dozing again and this created a soothing intimacy. 'My son works for my brother in Arezzo and we live in Florence. He has to be up at five every morning to get his train and you can imagine how exhausted he is coming back in the evenings. He's said to me many a time: —Mum, I'm sure I snored all the way and I think I was even dribbling a bit. If I ever met a nice girl on the train—I mean, can you imagine?'

The marshal fished out a big white handkerchief and dabbed at the corner of his mouth.

'A bit more to the side,' she murmured. 'That's it. Of course, he's lucky in many ways. My brother has a small goldsmithing factory there and it's not easy to find a job these days, is it?'

'It's not.' He prayed that she'd go on talking and not leave him alone with that dream.

'Of course, we've thought about a car—he's only ever had a moped—but it's still a long journey, he'd still have to be off very early, and what's snoring on the train compared to the risks of driving on the motorway half asleep?'

'You're quite right. The motorways are dangerous enough when we're wide awake. You make him stick to the train.' He dried his eyes and put his sunglasses on.

'I can see the sun's bothering you.'

'It's nothing. Just an allergy.' But wanting her to go on talking and afraid the black glasses might put her off, he said, 'I have two boys myself.' That kept them going for a quarter of an hour or so.

Then she offered, 'You must think it odd, my travelling back up to Florence at this hour—though my sister-in-law's a lot better—but I've got workmen coming at eight this morning and I really didn't want to put them off because I've been waiting weeks. You know what it's like . . .'

It was the third time she'd opened up this space for him to talk about the reason for his night journey.

He told her, instead, about his recent experience with builders and the pink tiles.

'No! You must have been furious!'

As long as she kept talking . . . He could tell

that she knew what he needed and that her attempts to give him a cue were born of sympathy, not idle curiosity.

They were approaching the outskirts of Florence. She offered him a sweet.

'Thank you.'

'They're fruit jellies. Sometimes you need a bit of sugar to buck you up. It's been a long night.'

'Yes.'

'Not many people come up from Rome on this train now there's the Intercity that's so much faster.'

'It was the first one leaving and I was tired, so . . .'

Reluctant to break this invisible thread connecting him to a safe, sane world, he carried her small case to the taxi rank. A carabinieri car was waiting for him across the way in the cold dawn light of the empty station square. He held the car door for her and, since there was nothing else he could say, he said, 'Thank you.'

*   *   *

'I want his body brought back to Florence. I want Forli to do the autopsy.' He offered no explanation.

The captain asked for none. All he said was, 'The Roman magistrate would never allow that.'

179

The marshal's thoughts were still wandering in a velvety Roman night. Two feathery palms lit by yellow globes of light outside a family trattoria. A cheery waiter in a red striped waistcoat signalling to him as he stood on the cobbles ringing a brass doorbell, telling him the man he was looking for was down here eating with his girlfriend. Eleven-thirty at night and it was still hot. Inside the trattoria, someone was playing a mandolin and singing as waiters called out orders to the smoky kitchen. Inside the marshal's head, Esposito's face looked in two different directions and when they moved him stuff slopped about. The heat and the lights made the scene in front of him too unreal, too theatrical, to cancel out the other and he longed to get away from Rome . . .

Now, he forced himself to concentrate on today, on this quiet office, on what the captain was saying. 'I could try for it on the grounds that we need his DNA as part of an ongoing investigation into the Japanese girl's death—'

'Akiko.'

I'm sorry?'

'Nothing. Her name is Akiko. Akiko Kametsu.'

'Yes, of course.'

'I want Forli to do the autopsy. Her name . . . I kept forgetting it. It just came into my head that those films they show on television sometimes about real crimes or stuff about the war . . . when they say this is a true story, only some names have been changed to protect the innocent. I used to wonder about that. Who are they, the innocent? How do you separate them off so cleanly? And now I can see it—oh, not the way they mean it when they say it on television. None of us can be said to be as innocent as that. It's just a different way of . . . a different world. All the people involved in this case . . . Akiko herself, the artisans, Esposito . . . They're the innocent, you see, and yet there's nobody else, so—'

'Guarnaccia, you're exhausted. What possessed you to travel up in the middle of the night when you could have stayed over I don't know, but there was certainly no reason to come straight here from the station—have you even had breakfast?'

'Breakfast . . . no. No, I don't think so . . .' There was a lingering sweetness in his mouth but he didn't remember having had a coffee.

'Go home, Guarnaccia, and get some sleep.'

'Yes. Esposito's mother called him Enzo. I know I'm not explaining myself. It's just that I'm seeing things in a different way now.'

'You're tired. But I do understand that you're also upset. There's nothing to be done now except forget what's been a very bad business. You liked Esposito. So did I. I had high hopes of him. But at least his death extinguishes the crime. We can only let his memory rest and go on.'

181

'No, no . . . Death doesn't extinguish the crime in his mother's mind. We have to protect the innocent, don't we? I understand who they are now and I've got to find whoever it is who isn't one of them. I want his body brought back here because Professor Forli can help me.'

'I've said I'll try but I'm not hopeful, I'm really not. I keep telling you to go home and you're not moving.'

'No. I'm sorry.' He knew what he must look like. Lorenzini had told him often enough:

—Sitting there, crouched like a bulldog making up its mind to sink its teeth into somebody's leg. Sometimes your breathing's that deep and slow I think you must actually be growling—and God help the owner of the leg you sink your teeth into. Can't you just ask for a warrant like anybody else?

How can you just ask for a warrant when you don't know whose name should be on it? The captain was too polite, too formal, to make the sort of comments Lorenzini came out with but the marshal said again, 'I'm sorry. You see my only hope was this friend in Rome. And now . . .'

'You're sure his alibi will be confirmed?'

'There's no doubt. He was in Japan for his brother's wedding. He showed me digital photographs and his passport. He said he was worried about Akiko because she'd been down to see him just before he left. They met here in Florence when they were both studying art

182

history—his name is Toshimitsu . . . I've written his surname down . . .'

'It doesn't matter now. It'll be in your report. Go on.'

'He works for a restorer now They were good friends, nothing more. He said they kept in touch. He said:

—Then she got pregnant and didn't know what to do.

—Perhaps I was the only person she could talk to because I understood what she'd got away from.

—She said the Easter visit to Naples had been a disaster. Enzo's family suffocated her. They never got a minute to themselves and everything they did was organised for them. She said he couldn't see it. He thought it was normal and it didn't bother him at all that they were told where to go, how to dress, who to invite back and what was to be eaten. He and his mother even talked over buying a flat and she wasn't included in the conversation. When she heard about it, she objected. Peruzzi had offered to help with a deposit. He wouldn't hear of that, to be helped by a stranger instead of family, while she would have preferred it. She was often in tears but they couldn't even have a quarrel because there was no privacy. For her, he was a different person from the man she'd fallen in love with. She felt she didn't know him at all. They quarrelled on the train back to Florence and she broke it off. But it turned out she was already pregnant. The last time she called me she had decided on an abortion. She said her sister had pressurised her, telling her not to lose her feedom and ruin her life, to use her intelligence. After all, what had she run away from her family for? Akiko said she was right. It was the only sensible thing to do but she was so distressed . . . It seems her sister had talked to their mother about it—it was out of the question to let their father find out. The mother said she must abort the child quickly and come back home. As long as it was kept quiet there was no harm done and she was still young enough to make a respectable match. Respectable, meaning lucrative.

—When was this, do you remember?

—Yes, I do. She called me on the eighth of May and she was booked in at the hospital the next day, the day I left for Tokyo. I wish I hadn't had to go. She was really suffering, desperate, even. She could hardly speak for crying and she apologised for calling me in that state. Some people, I know, have an abortion without thinking twice but if they love the father . . .

—If you'd seen them together, you'd understand. They came to stay with us for two days once and—I don't know how to put it— they kind of lit up everything around them. It affected everybody who saw them, even Mario in the trattoria downstairs. He offered us a bottle of spumante to toast them.

—Agli innamorati!

—I don't think they drank more than a sip. They were drunk with each other and so innocent, like two children.

'I'm sure his concern was genuine, Captain. He was very shocked when I told him what had happened to her. He protested:

—You surely don't think that Enzo . . . ?

—I don't know.

—When I got back from Tokyo, he was waiting for me. Mario, who has the trattoria downstairs, said he'd been hanging around for days, waiting for me. Mario keeps my spare keys and knew when I'd be back. If you'd seen the state he was in . . .

—I did see.

—Of course, yes. Anyway, Mario was worried. He said, I don't mind telling you, he frightened me. Asked me if his little girlfriend had been here—well, of course, I'd seen her but I said no. The man looked dangerous. It's none of my business but if there's something going on between you and that Japanese girlfriend of his you'd better watch your back. I said there wasn't, that he was upset because she'd left him, that was all. You watch your back, anyway, he said, because I've seen a thing or two in my time and that man's about to do something drastic. Well, he was right. When I opened the door to Enzo next morning, there was no denying it. His face was

185

white and his eyes burning. He said to me, I know she must have come here. There's nowhere else. She came here, didn't she?

—He looked shocking. I said he should come in, sit down and try and calm himself. I said that once she got over the abortion they would have time to think things out. I said, However bad it seems now, it's not the end of the world. She was frightened, can't you understand? She felt trapped. But she loves you, I'm sure of it. You'll convince her in the end if you just keep calm. You'll get married. There'll be other children. I wish you'd come in, let me make you a coffee, or something.

—But he wouldn't. I don't think he was even listening to me. All he said was, She must have hated me. Remembering his face then, it's easy to imagine he would have killed himself. When he left here, he was like somebody walking about in a waking nightmare. He can't have done that to her. He can't, can he?

The marshal paused, staring at Captain Maestrangelo, willing him to understand. But he was in a waking nightmare himself and he couldn't explain.

They would have been all right. They were so young and they needed help. She was so far from her home and only had this friend Toshimitsu to tell. He couldn't advise her, but at least she could talk to him in her own language, couldn't she? And it's true what he

186

said, that he knew what she'd run away from. Esposito didn't and his mother didn't either. The world's changed so much, so fast. We're not able to help our children, that's the problem. They were so young . . . When we're older, settled in our lives, we know what we can cope with and even if things go wrong we can be less catastrophic . . . his face was split right up the middle . . . it's going to be hard to forget that . . . and still, life goes on . . .'

'Guarnaccia,' interrupted the captain, 'don't you think you should get some sleep, clear your head?'

'No. He told me how Akiko and Enzo met. I wanted to know that—after all, they came from such different worlds. It seems a group of lads from the non-commissioned officers' school went on a jaunt to the Japanese restaurant when it first opened but that, since they serve Italian food as well, almost all of them lost their courage and ordered pasta. One or two of them, Esposito among them, had a go at ordering something Japanese. Akiko was at the next table, celebrating her birthday with Issino. Since she spoke good Italian, she was asked by the proprietor to help out. She tried to teach him to use chopsticks.

'She started off showing him how to hold them but he was hopeless and they were laughing. So, she placed her hand on the back of his to guide him. They stopped laughing. He just looked at her. That was all it took.

'He told me how Akiko changed:

—She was never the sentimental type and if she'd ever been in love before she certainly never mentioned it. She said to me, Everything's different now.

'I'm sure if they hadn't gone down to Naples she would have been all right. After all, he wasn't living at home, he was in the army. They could have made their own life.

'He seemed to me', the marshal said, 'to be taking Akiko's story very badly, considering their relationship, and I was right. The girlfriend he'd introduced me to in the trattoria before we came up to his apartment to talk was American and they were in a crisis because she wanted them to go and live in California once she'd finished her year here and he felt he needed to be in Rome because of his work. I tried to reassure him but he wasn't convinced. He said:

—You think you've found the perfect person as long as you're just in love and living in a sort of vacuum. Then you start talking about marriage and suddenly it's not just about two people any more.'

The captain got to his feet and started to walk about the room. The marshal, supersensitive as he was in his tired and distressed state, felt his agitation and the cause of it. Again, as in Rome, he tried to reassure. 'It needn't have ended like it did, it wouldn't have ended like it did. They would have talked. They would have found a way through. People get over their problems if they love each other.'

Behind him, he heard the captain stop, then stride back towards his desk. He rang the bell. 'They don't get over death. I'll have some coffee brought for you. Then you're going home.'

*   *   *

Teresa tried to send him straight to bed but he didn't go. He didn't tell her so but he was afraid of going to sleep because if he went to sleep, the nightmare would come back. What was worse, he would yet again wake up to find that what happened in the nightmare had really happened and the only part that wasn't true was the part about everything being all right, about Esposito walking beside him, comforted, healed. That really was a dream. He would be obliged to face the nightmare and the worse awakening when it came to bedtime, but at least Teresa would be there. He wasn't going to fall asleep alone if he could avoid it. Teresa look hard at his face. She didn't argue with him.

'Well, at least let Lorenzini deal with everything. You're in no fit state. And come home early. I'll make you a good meal and then you can watch the news and have an afternoon nap on the sofa.'

He didn't say anything, only looked at her, pleading in silence.

'I've those jeans of Totò's I've promised to shorten, so you'll keep me company. Now have a shower and get into uniform. You'll feel more yourself.'

*   *   *

Back in uniform, feeling more himself, the marshal stayed in his office and dealt with every available scrap of dull, blessedly normal paperwork as he waited for Lorenzini to finish 'dealing with everything' and join him. When he came in and sat down, he wanted details of Esposito's suicide. He didn't get them. It wasn't squeamishness. It wasn't distress. It was a question of concentration. He didn't know how he was going to get where he was going, only that he had to go there and there was so little time.

Lorenzini had to help him. 'You mean you refuse to believe—even now that he's killed himself, even though he lied about his mother and went missing . . .'

'I'm not interested in believing things or not believing things.'

'And what about the facts in the case? Are you not interested in those either?'

'The facts . . . yes. You see, you're better at those things than I am.'

'What do you mean?'

'I don't know exactly what I mean except that now I've got another date, apart from May twenty-first when Peruzzi last saw her. The ninth of May. Going by what her friend— Toshimitsu—told me, that was the date she booked for the abortion.'

'Easy enough to check round the hospitals, then. There'll be a paper trail, even if she didn't turn up.'

'Yes. She couldn't go through with it because she loved him. Between the ninth and the twenty-first she must have been so distressed . . . I haven't a lot of time. I want this sorted out before the funeral. It's too big a burden for his mother. Losing her only son, suicide, an accusation of murder.'

'Death extinguishes the crime.'

'Not for her. The papers will put two and two together.'

'While you . . .'

Had he been wanting to say: —While you won't?—It didn't matter.

'You understand me? There's no time.'

'If you want me to deal with checking the hospitals, of course I will.'

'Yes. But help me. I have to find someone . . .'

'Out of thin air.'

'Yes. I need more facts, maybe more dates.'

He had to keep on at Lorenzini until he came up with what he needed. There was nothing he could ask for exactly because he didn't know what he was after, only that Lorenzini was the one who had to provide it. He stared at him, dogged, insistent. That irritated, almost pitying look meant he was getting there.

'Well, dates would be something—I don't know about plucking a suspect out of thin air for you but they might well result in an alibi for Esposito, given that his movements are all recorded here. If his mother's your only worry, that would be enough, wouldn't it?'

'I don't know . . .'

'All right. You want your phantom suspect behind bars.'

The marshal brooded on this a moment, staring past Lorenzini at the map on the opposite wall and a tiny piazza with no name.

'Yes,' he said at last. He couldn't explain just who and what he felt the need to protect, even to himself. 'But you're right. To start by proving Esposito's innocence would be something . . . Only, Forli can't give me a precise time of death, just a rough idea of the number of days. In water it's not easy. The fish . . .'

—It's because I have no face. —He could still hear her voice, so cold and sad. He hadn't even remembered her name. She was just 'the Japanese girl'. He still couldn't shake off the nightmare. It was more real than anything around him. He must try to listen to Lorenzini.

'So, if you put Forli's estimate together with the day Peruzzi last saw her—I mean, you might not need the exact time if Esposito was on duty all day. It had to happen in the daytime if it happened in the gardens. Esposito was here inside already, but the girl, even if she'd fixed to meet him, wouldn't have been allowed through the gates anywhere near closing time.'

'No.'

'So ask Peruzzi. If she left the workshop when it closed, half past seven or something, to go home, then the Boboli Gardens were already shut and you're talking about the next day and Forli's estimate should be enough. I'll check the daily sheets for you and any reports with Esposito's name on them.'

'Yes. Thanks.'

'So: Forli's estimate, opening hours of the Boboli Gardens, Esposito's movements. If there's an alibi there, I'll find it for you but if there isn't . . . the scene's so close by and if there's even half an hour of Esposito's time unaccounted for . . .'

Lorenzini was getting to his feet.

'Wait.' He had to make him stay. He needed more. 'I was wondering how things were going with . . .' With what? He must keep him there. Pictures flipped around in his weary head, a kaleidoscope of useless images: a builder trundling through clouds of cigarette smoke, that awful woman with the handbag and her skewed eye-shadow, a duty rosta for the medieval football, Nardi—'Nardi.'

'What about him?'

'Nothing. I've been leaving you to deal with so much. I just wondered how that was going.'

'Oh. It's all calming down. I think I've pretty well got to the bottom of the problem. I talked to the butcher and their neighbours . . .'

Keep talking . . . just keep talking . . . That was his brain, slopping about . . . he was so clever and now his brain . . .

'Anyway, there's one woman—I don't know if you know her but she's not bad looking. She doesn't look so much like a housewife from around here as like Claudia Cardinale playing the part of a housewife in a film, if you know what I mean. Funnily enough, she is called Claudia.'

'I know her. She's a beautiful woman who always looks worn-out. Always wears down-at-heel shoes. Married to a short fat chap who looks twice her age.'

Two halves looking two different ways . . . If he let his mind drift, he felt as though he were still on the train, his body feeling the rhythm. Was he falling asleep? Listen to Lorenzini.

'And she told me she's been following the whole story. She said:

—It's better than any soap opera, I can tell you. I missed most of the fight but I managed to get to the window in time to see them being separated and Monica leaving in an ambulance. Fancy calling the Misericordia for a scratch or two! Is she really going to go on

194

telly?

'I told her it wasn't our business, as long as it stayed out of the courts but that I hoped to put her off doing it, seeing as they'd all got on so well for so many years except for a bit of a quarrel every now and again.'

'And what did she think about it?'

Keep him talking. He mustn't go yet . . .

'That's just it. She said there'd been a bit of jealousy at first but Monica and Costanza had got used to each other years ago and even get together, now and again, to talk over his faults—he was drinking a bit too much at one time but they soon put a stop to that between them.'

'Poor chap . . . Why don't you sit down?'

'I can't. It's late and I ought to be getting home—and didn't you say your wife was expecting you early? It's after one. Anyway, I've started so I'll finish. She said this fight was different. She said it's not about love, it's about money.'

The marshal stood up, his gaze still fixed on Lorenzini. 'Money? What money? I didn't know any of them had any money.'

'No, but Nardi has a pension, a pretty decent pension after working on the railways all his life.'

'So?'

'So Monica's claiming half of it. She says he spends as much time in her house, using her hot water, her heating, her electricity, as he

195

does in his own—which isn't quite true—and as much time in her bed as in Costanza's—which is. Of course, Monica has her mother's old age pension now but her mother's nearly ninety. She has to think of the future. She has a point, you know. It must be twenty years they've been together.'

'Yes, but—'

'Monica didn't need to stay a widow. She could have married three times over, they say.'

'I don't doubt it. What I can't understand is what any woman could see in Nardi.'

'They say he looks better with his teeth in.'

'But he never puts them in!'

'No. Anyway, what Costanza says is that if his pension—or half of it—goes, he goes. Hence the scrap.'

'Hmph. I have to go. Teresa . . .'

He left Lorenzini standing there. He was vaguely aware of the puzzled frown that followed him but it didn't matter. He had to get on. He was still exhausted and still upset about Esposito, but under all that, deep inside, he was now calm.

CHAPTER NINE

The chatter at table flowed around him,
comforting. He felt Teresa watching him but
she didn't bother him at all, except to say every
so often in a gentle voice, 'Salva . . .'

'What?'

This was because the boys were asking him
something, looking at him, expecting an
answer.

'We'll see . . .' was all he could manage. And
sometimes, 'Ask your mother . . .'

Later, they took their coffee through and
settled on the cool leather sofa in the drawing
room to watch the news. He leaned back
and dozed a little, always aware of the
newsreader's urgent voice. He was aware, too,
of the small movements Teresa was making as
she sewed beside him. Sometimes he was
rocked by the train in a weary journey that
went on and on and on, but when his head fell
sideways it touched Teresa's warm bare arm
and he was comforted. He woke after almost
an hour, refreshed. The two boys were waiting
outside the drawing-room door, having been
told to keep quiet because their dad had been
up all night. They were still quiet but staring at
him, their eyes hopeful. What did they want?

'Mum says we can but not on our own. She
says only if you take us.'

It was Giovanni talking and that was odd. Totò was always the ringleader when they were planning something—but what was it?

'We wanted to go with everybody from school. There's a whole gang . . . Mum says the final's too dangerous because there's always a fight afterwards.'

The medieval football, then.

'Hmph.'

'But we can if you take us.'

'All right, we'll see.'

'Oh, Dad! You always say we'll see, and it's San Giovanni! It's my birthday—and my name day and the Whites are playing and we've never been to the final, ever!'

'I know. We'll talk about it later.' He was opening the bedroom door to go and get changed but a voice in his head stopped him.

—If you don't water a plant, it dies. It can't wait.

That's what it was—Totò was there, a little boy again, at least for a moment. He wasn't taking the lead but he was there, supporting his brother, wanting something from his dad, no longer shut in the bedroom, crying.

So he placed a big hand on the shoulder of each and promised, 'I'll get tickets—but for all of us, your mum as well, because we're going to go to Lapo's place for a good meal first.'

'With cake and spumante after?' Giovanni's dark eyes became as huge as the marshal's own.

198

'Of course with cake and spumante after. It's your birthday and your name day, isn't it? And now let me get changed and go back to work.'

*　　*　　*

There were no windows in Lapo's small back room, so the lamps were on, illuminating the paintings by local artists, rows of bottles on the shelves, stacks of white plates. Even so, the circles of yellow light they gave out weren't strong and the corners remained shadowy. The pushed-back tables with only their dark-green undercloths and the solemn faces looking at the marshal gave a funereal air to the gathering. Lapo had rounded up anybody from the square who wanted to come and now he offered a glass of vin santo to everyone. At this odd afternoon hour, the room smelled only of wine stains, cigarette smoke and coffee.

'The marshal says they'll eventually send our little Akiko back to her family in Japan so this is a bit of a farewell gathering for her. She always liked vin santo. Now, let's hear what the marshal has to tell us.'

'Well, I'd better tell you first of all that I've been up all night, so you'll forgive me if I'm a bit . . . it's been an upsetting business, too, I know you'll understand that . . . Anyway, if I'm not making myself clear, you only have to ask.'

The men wore grey or black cotton coats,

199

aprons, overalls. Santini's hair was tied back with the usual bit of rag.

He scanned their faces, those close to him that he could see properly, those behind in the shadows. There was still some diffidence there, he could feel it, but they were listening. They were giving him a chance. So, he planted his big hands squarely on his knees and began. 'I know a lot of you must have thought I was trying to keep Esposito's name out of this. Some of you were even understanding about it and very discreet. I couldn't see it at the time but I want to thank you for that now, for your trust, I mean. You relied on me to do the right thing and when I didn't, well . . . you felt let down. So for those of you I haven't said this to already, I didn't know about Esposito and Akiko. I can only ask you to believe that. If you don't . . .

'He hadn't been with us all that long. When you live in barracks you're cut off from old friends back at home, from your family. You can't be on familiar terms with the men you command . . .'

The next bit was difficult but he was determined to say it. He took a sip of the vin santo, which he didn't want and could ill afford to drink in his exhausted state. 'I wish . . . I'd have liked to think he could have confided in me, but these are delicate matters and maybe he thought I wouldn't understand. Maybe he thought I was too old. Anyway, he didn't confide in anyone—he didn't confide in me. Now he's dead. You'll have seen that on last night's news and—though they didn't say it in so many words because there has to be an autopsy and so on—we think he killed himself.'

Some discreet murmurs, a scraped chair, a loud voice: 'But did he kill Akiko?'

'What are you on about? He wanted to marry her!'

'No, no. He's right. The question has to he asked. The marshal knows that and he'll think no worse of us for asking.'

'What do you know about it?'

'Let him finish! We've all got work to do!'

The marshal waited until they'd shouted each other down and seemed ready to listen. He, too, had work to do but he was all quiet inside now and moving steadily forward. He had to satisfy their curiosity about Esposito's death and then listen to what they could tell him. He coughed and the last mutterings died down.

'As far as I can piece it together, what happened was that Esposito was given leave to go home to Naples and visit his mother.' He had to be honest with them. He didn't want to say it but he needed their trust and, this way, they had to give it to him. 'He'd told us his mother was ill. It wasn't true.'

More murmurs, but nobody ventured to comment on that. It had worked. Any diffidence had melted. They gazed at him now like children being told a story.

'He took the train for Naples, as he'd said he would, but he got off it in Rome. Given the lie he told us about his mother, we have to think that he always intended to do that. He went looking for a friend of Akiko's. He was very agitated and, according to the friend, he said nothing much other than "It's all over." Some of you may have known that Akiko was expecting a child. Although she didn't go through with it, she had planned on an abortion. This all makes things look very bad for Esposito, I realise that, but I hope now you'll believe that nobody's trying to cover anything up here.'

He paused and glanced at Peruzzi. Most of the men in the room turned to look at him, too. He had taken care to inform Peruzzi about everything before the others arrived, mindful of his heart condition. Things had to be done in the proper order, smooth and steady. Even so, when he'd first heard it all, Peruzzi had been obliged to sit down, his face pale.

—Oh, no . . . an abortion, no. She must have known that wasn't the answer.

—Yes, I think she did. Her friend in Rome said she was upset. Very upset.

—Hours and hours she sat there working and tears were dropping on her hands. Hours and hours . . . And no wonder. She couldn't

202

tell me. A girl needs her mother . . .

'Hmph.' The marshal didn't go into that.

Now, Peruzzi remained still and silent, looking down at his hands. The other men turned their attention back to the marshal's story.

Lapo's wife, in her white apron and cook's hat, was leaning against the doorway of the lighted kitchen, listening too.

—He was missing for some days. That was because Akiko's friend—whose name is Toshimitsu—was away. He'd gone to Tokyo for a wedding. Esposito hung around in Rome, waiting. We don't know yet where he stayed. When Toshimitsu got back he tried to calm Esposito down but it did no good.'

'So why did he kill himself?'

'Out of remorse, of course! Because he killed her, didn't he?'

'You don't know that! How can you know that?'

'He wanted to marry her, for God's sake. You don't suddenly up and murder somebody when you want to marry them!'

'What about her threatening an abortion? What about that? Any man would be upset. That could have done it, am I right, Marshal?'

'How can he know that? Whose child was it, that's the point.'

'Come on! We knew Akiko!'

'You hadn't eaten a kilo of salt with her, as they say. You never know with people—I

203

mean, what about this chap, whats-his-name, in Rome. How do we know it wasn't his, if she went running to him?'

'Shut up!'

'I'm just saying, that's all. She wouldn't be the first—'

'Shut up!'

The marshal let them shout until one particular nuisance—a man in glasses whom he'd never seen before and who had clearly never spoken a word to Akiko—had been silenced.

'After that, Esposito boarded the Naples train . . . yesterday morning.' It seemed so long ago but it was only yesterday. It didn't seem real, either, when he tried to tell it, because it felt more like he was recounting his nightmare.

'The train had been travelling for something like ten minutes when, according to witnesses, Esposito left his seat very suddenly. His fellow passengers said he looked wretched, as though he were going to be sick. Somebody said:

—We thought maybe he had a hangover, that he was still drunk, even, because he looked as though he didn't know where he was.

'They all remembered that he made a sort of noise as he lurched out of his seat. Some said he was starting to vomit and others said it was more like a groan or a sob. He locked himself into the lavatory. A lot of people heard the shot. There was blood coming out under the door. Somebody pulled the emergency cord. It took some time before the door was broken down. He'd shot himself in the face. They couldn't do anything to help him. He was already dead.'

When the marshal stopped speaking, there was silence. Seeing that they were moved and knowing that their defence would be some cynical crack that would break the spell, he filled the silence himself. 'Esposito was the only son of a widow, so you can imagine that she . . . I shouldn't be telling you any of this so don't, for God's sake, tell anybody you heard it from me because I'll deny it. Are we clear on that?'

The critical moment passed and they were soon shouting each other down about who had seen Esposito and who hadn't.

'No, no, no! Ask Peruzzi. His hair was black.'

'I'm telling you I saw him waiting for her outside the workshop.'

'You saw no such thing. He only ever showed up here once and that was when she'd already disappeared. Am I right, Peruzzi?'

'Yes. The day before the marshal came round, asking the same questions.'

'So that was the day I saw him.'

'Well he wasn't waiting for Akiko then, was he, since she'd already gone!'

'How was I to know who he was waiting for? I'm just saying I saw him, that's all. I'm just saying. I think he was wearing a leather overcoat.'

'What leather overcoat? What leather overcoat? In May! He was in uniform, Peruzzi said. You're talking rubbish! Shut up, for Christ's sake!'

There was always somebody ready to be convinced they'd seen whatever ought to have been seen, especially if there was the chance of saying it on the television news. The self-styled witness had a raucous voice but the others formed a chorus to shout him down and the small room rang with their din. Lapo's wife retreated into her kitchen. The marshal made no attempt to restore order and quiet. He only ducked his head below the level of all the shouting faces and gesticulating arms to catch the eye of Santini who was sitting in silence behind a table a little to his right.

The marshal spoke in almost a whisper to make himself heard below the shouting. 'You saw him, didn't you?'

Did Santini hear or lip-read? In either case he nodded.

'In uniform?'

The marshal signalled to him and touched Peruzzi's arm.

They moved into the front room which was just as small but where there was daylight and they could distance themselves from the strident polemic.

'So you two are the only ones to have seen

Esposito, the day before I came round asking about Akiko. Is that right? And you said to me yesterday morning, didn't you, Santini, that he was in uniform.'

'Yes, but he didn't speak to me. I just saw him go into Peruzzi's.'

'And you, Peruzzi, you were so angry with me that first time because I came asking the same questions he'd already asked: I don't know where she is! How many more of you do I have to tell? Isn't that what you shouted at me?'

'I don't remember. She'd gone and I was angry.'

'But you told him she might be in Rome, or even Tokyo, like you said?'

'I can't remember! I was upset!'

'Try not to get upset now. Sit down. That's better. Try to think back. Did he ask you if you knew where she'd gone?'

'No!'

'What, then?'

'Nothing! He didn't ask me anything. I knew he must be looking for her. Of course he was looking for her. What else would he come to me for? I told him the only place I could think of was Rome, the same as I told you, and if she wasn't there, she'd gone back to where she came from. I couldn't help him. And he just stood there looking like somebody had hit him with a brick. He just stood there!'

'He didn't ask you anything? He didn't say

anything?'

'I'm telling you! He just stood there!'

'All right. Calm down. Please, calm down. He must have presented himself, said who he was at least, if you'd never met him before.'

'I knew who he was! I've seen a dozen photographs of him—not that he looked much like them that day. He looked like a dead man then. It's no surprise to me if he . . . He didn't speak a word. His eyes . . . She talked about him all the time. She said he was thoughtful, tender, warm-hearted, and she was too intelligent to be mistaken, I'd swear to that.'

'Peruzzi, listen. I have to ask you something that's very important now that I know about Esposito: Can you remember what time she left the workshop on the last day you saw her? Was it your usual closing time?'

'Closing time? No, of course not, it was eleven thirty in the morning.'

'Eleven thirty in the morning? Where was she going? Where was she going at that time of the morning?'

'To the bank.'

'For herself or for you?'

'For me, of course. It was Friday. She always took the cash and cheques in on Friday mornings. Ever since my heart attack, she—'

'Peruzzi, this is important. I'm trying to work out exactly when this happened. I need to know her movements and Esposito's.'

'She used to meet him sometimes for a

quick coffee, if he was out and about. She always went to the bank at the same time—I'm not getting him into trouble saying that, am I?'

'You can't get him into trouble now, Peruzzi.'

'No. No, of course not—but I'm not saying she was going to meet him that day. She didn't say she was.'

'And would she have said?'

'I . . . Maybe, maybe not, but this was after, after the upset . . .' Peruzzi fell silent.

'All right. But did she get there? Did she get to the bank and deposit the money?'

'I don't know.'

'You don't know? How can you not know that? You'd have noticed that nothing was deposited for the whole week, wouldn't you?'

'No! But my son would have found out, if not right away then at the end of the month when he looked at my accounts. You're never accusing Akiko of—'

'I'm not accusing Akiko of anything. Don't you realise that, if somebody knew she was carrying money every Friday, she could have been robbed? There was nothing in her handbag to tell us she was going to or coming from a bank. No money, no cheques and no bank receipt either. I presume she gave you the receipts?'

'Yes . . . well, she filed them until it was time to do my tax declaration. Anyway, what do you mean, robbed? She might have been robbed in the street but she . . .' He stopped himself, blocking off the obvious conclusion that the marshal would like to block, too.

It was Santini who said it. 'She must have met whoever it was, up there.'

'She didn't say she was meeting him. She didn't say. I'd have remembered, wouldn't I? I mean, when she didn't come back, I'd have thought . . .'

'I suppose you bank in Piazza Pitti like all the other artisans around here?'

'Yes—I won't believe it. Whatever you find out, I won't believe it of Esposito. She knew him better than anybody—better than you, if you'll excuse me saying so—and she trusted him. That's enough for me.' His colour was bad. He was holding his chest now.

The marshal laid a steadying hand on his shoulder, 'Think about your health.'

'If he killed her, I'll never trust anything or anybody again, and especially not myself. If he killed her . . .'

Santini looked at the marshal. 'He didn't, did he?'

'I don't know. Go back in there and break it up. I have to get on.'

He left them.

Money. But Esposito? He wasn't convinced. He wasn't convinced at all, but he was going on along this same road because, wherever it led, he knew it was the right road and he remained calm and clear-headed. He hadn't even forgotten that he had intended to mention Giovanni's birthday supper to Lapo. He could telephone later. Now he must speak to Captain Maestrangelo and then get to the bank.

'A warrant?' The captain looked relieved. Was that because the marshal in his present mood annoyed him? Or because he, too, was concerned to clear Esposito's name? He would never say and what did it matter? 'You're on to something, then?'

'No. Yes. It's about money. I want a search warrant to look into Peruzzi's accounts.'

'Peruzzi's accounts . . .? Do you have evidence of some irregularity on his part? You've been in touch with the Finance Police?'

'No. He told me he never bothered with bank stuff, you see. He left his son, who's an accountant, to fill in his tax returns and so on but it was Akiko who deposited his money.'

'That's all very well but he was running a business. There must have been day-to-day matters—'

'Akiko. Akiko was the one who did that. He wanted her to take over as manager one day. He was ill. She went to the bank, with the week's takings, every Friday. That's where she was going the last time he saw her.'

'Then you suspect her?'

'No.'

'No? Then what's all this about?'

'If I did suspect her, that would be reason

211

enough for a warrant, wouldn't it.' He stared hard at the captain, willing him to do it.

'I understand. And your real reason?'

'It's about money. I don't know . . . I need to have those accounts. I came to you rather than asking the prosecutor myself. You'll explain better, get it done quickly. I'm going to the bank now. Lorenzini can collect the warrant and follow me. Excuse me . . . I want to catch the manager before he leaves.' As he reached the door, he paused a moment. 'Esposito's body?'

'I've tried but I really don't think—you could talk to Forli. He might have an unofficial chat to whoever in Rome does the autopsy.'

'That's not . . . No, no.'

But in the car going back across the river to the bank, he did call Forli, just because it was something he could do, some way of not losing time. He felt like he'd felt in his dream as Akiko drifted away from him and his legs felt like they were made of lead.

'I wanted you to do the autopsy . . .' What could he say? Because you would talk to the dead man whose handsome face looked two different ways . . . He was too tired to think of any sort of reason at all.

Luckily, Forli was never too concerned about the other half of any conversation. 'I'll make a call to Rome, if you like, but you already know the only two things that matter: that he killed himself in Rome, for a start. We

212

get a lot of these cases in a year, you know that. They're invariably on Shakespearean lines, wouldn't you say?'

'I'm sorry, I . . .'

'Romeo didn't pop off to Rome to stab himself, when he found his girl dead, did he? His body was found with Juliet's in that tomb in Verona. And Othello didn't murder his Desdemona and then rush off to Rome to stab himself! Well, did he?'

'No.' What was this about? Verdi, at least, he could cope with. He tried to stop Forli rushing on. 'No. He killed himself in Desdemona's bedroom.'

'In Venice. Exactly. You must have dealt with a good few of these lovers' murder-suicide type cases.'

'One or two. You're right, of course. But you said I knew two things. That he killed himself in Rome—'

'And that he killed himself at all! Exactly! People don't commit suicide because of something distressing that happens to them—the human race would die out at that rate—they commit suicide because they're suicidal. Are his parents alive?'

'His father's dead.'

'Find out how. When you brought Esposito to my office before we'd identified the girl's body he'd didn't look too chipper—I remember looking closely at him, trying to remember who he was but once we were talking technical details he perked up no end and he'd have stayed around to see her lungs, if you'd let him. Think about that. We didn't know who she was then but if he killed her, he did, right? I can't imagine what good my doing the autopsy would be. He put a bullet through his brain with his own Beretta, as I heard it. What more do you want to know? You'd do better to talk to his family doctor.'

'His family doctor?'

'Or his mother. There'll be a history there. A brilliant student but too intense. None of the resilience you need in your line of work. "Let me have men about me that are fat, sleek-headed men and such as sleep a-nights." Like your good self, Marshal, eh?'

Fat . . . ? Overweight he admitted to, but he wasn't exactly fat. Solid, Teresa had once said, hugging him and laughing at him. Fat . . . that was a bit rude. The bit about sleeping at nights . . . chance'd be a fine thing. His vision, as he got out of the car in Piazza Pitti, was blurred with tiredness.

'Wait for me here—no.' Tread carefully, do things right, pay attention to every detail. Tiredness mustn't spoil things now. 'You can't park here in this heat. Go back up to the station and wait for me in the shade. I'll walk up.'

'Thanks, Marshal.'

The bank was closed to customers at that hour. He rang the bell. It was very quiet inside.

The counter clerks were doing their accounts. The marshal banked here himself and though it was always Teresa who went in, he knew the manager in the Piazza Pitti branch to say good morning to. He was an affable sort but he seemed worried, though not about Akiko.

'Peruzzi, yes . . . Come into my office. Make yourself comfortable. I'm glad to see you, Marshal, I don't mind telling you, because somebody's got to talk some sense into him. I know his son's tried and I've written him letter after letter. It can't go on—and what's he spending it on, that's what I want to know? It wasn't too bad up to the time he had his heart attack, though he was always overdrawn, but now he's spending like there's no tomorrow. Having said that . . . perhaps that's what he really feels. They say he actually died—that his heart stopped—and that he doesn't look too good now.'

'No. No, he doesn't.'

'I'm in a difficult position. Peruzzi's an institution in this Quarter, you know that. I've been as elastic as is possible. Overdraft, bigger overdraft, occasional loans—and we're covering his utility bills and debit card withdrawals, and so on, his basic necessities, but I'm getting flak from above at this point. They don't understand that if I give up on Peruzzi I'll risk losing all the other artisans who bank here. They're good clients, steady,

215

our core customers. You understand me.'

'Yes. I need to see his transactions for May.'

'His transactions . . . ? Pardon me, but . . . I was assuming his son had asked you to have a word. I can't—'

'No. I've asked for a warrant. I expect my second in command to arrive here with it any minute.' The captain wouldn't let him down. 'This is a murder inquiry. Peruzzi's apprentice was murdered in the Boboli Gardens on the twenty-first of May. She left the workshop that day, a Friday, to come here and deposit the week's takings. I need to know if she arrived here so . . .'

'A murder inquiry? I hadn't heard anything —it's true I've been away for two weeks' holiday . . .'

216

'It's not likely you'd have heard anything if you had been here. It barely made it into the news. We weren't able to identify her for a while. She had no documents in her bag and she had no money, no cheques and no receipt from this bank, either. But Peruzzi tells me she was coming here.'

'She was. She did come. It wasn't long before I went on holiday. I wouldn't be likely to forget it. I'd been worried about Peruzzi's financial situation, as I said, and since he never answered my letters—apparently he dumps anything from the bank on his son without even opening it—and since the son himself had told me he couldn't bring his father to his senses, I warned my staff to look out for the Japanese apprentice and send her in to see me.'

'So you spoke to her that morning?'

'I certainly did—oh, there wasn't a lot I could tell her because of confidentiality but, frankly, she was my last hope. His debts were such that I was faced with the prospect of foreclosing on his mortgage.'

'Mortgage . . . I thought he owned everything—surely, it was his father's before him? At least, so I've always heard.'

'You're right. They've been shoemakers for generations and certainly owned the place. He remortgaged about eight months ago.'

'Eight months . . .' After his heart attack. All

the images in the marshal's head were shifting, changing, going in and out of focus. He felt he was back where he started but with one difference. Not love but money . . .

'The son can't have been too pleased. I know he had no interest in taking over the business, let alone learning the trade, but it was his inheritance that was being spent, after all. How did he seem to you to be taking it?'

'Surprisingly well. Each time he came to see me about some bigger overdraft, loans, the remortgage, he was worried but never angry. After Peruzzi's illness, when things got suddenly worse, he said to me that his father had a very limited time left and that made it understandable that he should want to live life to the full. I tried to help him, discreetly. I said to him:

—I could refuse him this remortgage, you know. It's not a good idea and you have power of attorney. If you think . . .

—How can I refuse my father anything? He may only have months to live. Besides, if I refuse him what he wants he'll just take the power of attorney away, probably even quarrel with me, too. He has quite a temper. No, it's out of the question.

'Of course, when all's said and done, he's very comfortably off himself. He doesn't bank here—his offices are on the other side of the river in via de' Servi—but, frankly, an accountant with offices in via de' Servi—and a

218

home address on the Lungarno is doing well. And he has his father to thank for it. His father, after all, encouraged him to go to university, never complained that he didn't follow the family tradition.'

'No. He's very proud of his son. There was no quarrel there and, as you say, he has good reason to be grateful to his father and not want a quarrel now. Even so . . .' The marshal remained silent a while, watching the bank manager's pink fingers twirling a gold pen. 'Even so, it seems to me that there's a lot of money involved. I don't mind telling you—in confidence, that goes without saying, because I shouldn't really be telling you this—' There was no reason at all why not but the best way to gain somebody's confidence is to confide in them first. Or appear to. 'It crossed my mind that Peruzzi had become very fond of this young apprentice. I didn't know what terms their relationship was on, of course . . .

'Peruzzi? *Peruzzi?*'

'I know. I felt the same. But all that money was going somewhere. The only thing is, by all accounts she had no money to spend. She was also engaged to be married, to a young NCO from my station.'

'I see.'

'No. No, you don't see. I've had to face the fact that when she left him, as she did, he might have killed her. Nobody's trying to cover anything up here is what I'm trying to make

219

clear to you.'

'Of course not.'

'Hmph, well. I don't know about of course not. These things happen. But—and again, this is in confidence—the lad killed himself. Shot himself.'

'Not the one that was on the news?'

'Yes. His name was Esposito.'

'That's the one, yes—but that was in Rome, wasn't it? Was he running away? I seem to remember it happened in an airport, or something.'

'In the train. In Rome, yes. So, believe me, this is just about getting to the bottom of this young woman's death. Peruzzi, you see, wanted them to marry. He had offered to help them buy a house. I got the feeling he was lonely. His wife's dead, his son's gone his own way. Akiko married and pregnant, settled here, meant a family for him, someone to hand on his skill to, a whole new start. He couldn't disinherit his son by law, even did he want to, and it seems to me that his son's the light of his life—at least since he lost Akiko.'

'Akiko . . . ?'

'That's the young woman's name.'

'Ah, yes. Sweet little thing, very pretty.'

'I'm wondering if perhaps he was somehow investing money for her, maybe buying property in her name. So you see, I need to know what you said to her and how she reacted.'

'I didn't tell her much, how could I? It was far too delicate a matter. I can tell you that, if he was salting money away and she knew about it, she must have been a very cool customer indeed. She was perfectly calm and composed. I just told her I needed to see Peruzzi urgently and that he didn't answer my letters. She said:

'He doesn't like to come. He said to me I have to learn to be manager because when his son inherits the shop he won't want to run it. I file everything and in spring Mr Peruzzi's son comes to take the file away. Mr Peruzzi doesn't want to do this.

—I understand, but I must see him. It's very urgent. I can't give you confidential information, do you understand that?

—Yes.

—And you'll tell him to come and see me, that it's absolutely urgent?

—Yes.

'Of course she didn't.'

'She never got the chance,' the marshal said. 'Peruzzi never saw her again. She died that day, I think, though I'll probably never know for sure. Do you remember what time she left here?'

'Not precisely but . . .' He reached for his desk diary and turned back the pages. 'May . . . twenty-first. Here, I made a note. Peruzzi— that was to remind me to speak to the young woman and . . . yes, I had an appointment at

221

head office at twelve so she can't have been with me more than a quarter of an hour, if that . . . Oh, dear . . .'

'What is it?'

'I've just realised: as I say, I had an appointment. I showed her out of here and then I suppose I must have packed my briefcase. When I walked through to the main door she was still here, talking to someone who was holding her arm. I didn't think anything of it at the time but if something happened to her that day, as you say, then . . .'

'Were they quarrelling?'

'No . . . It was probably nothing.' The manager looked unhappy. It was clear he was wishing he hadn't spoken and now didn't know how to stop what he'd started.

'Something made you notice, even so.'

'As I said, she was a pretty little thing. I noticed her face was red, that's all. She was crying. She'd struck me as so calm and efficient before.'

'I see. And was the person she was talking to one of your customers?'

'No. No, he wasn't a customer. I don't know who he was. It only comes back to me because you said—well, he was wearing a carabiniere uniform. Possibly one or more members of my staff can confirm that. I'm sorry.'

The marshal sat there a moment in silence, hearing his own breathing. Some vague thoughts played around on the edge of his consciousness, such as that it's only too easy to let wishful thinking lead you away from the facts, that it didn't do to try to solve cases that you were emotionally involved in, that death extinguishes ... death extinguishes ...

Ideas that faded before they penetrated. His breathing deepened. He felt very quiet.

Somebody knocked and came in. It was a bank clerk with Lorenzini.

Before either of them could speak, the marshal stood up. 'I have to go.'

What was the matter with Lorenzini, staring like that?

'You've got the warrant? The manager here will give you a printout of all Peruzzi's transactions over the period he's been concerned about.'

'Yes but—I need to have a word with you—'

'Not now.' He turned to look at the manager and say, 'I imagine it must have crossed your mind that all this odd shifting about of money might be about avoiding death duties rather than enjoying life?'

'Yes. Naturally. Once he knew how ill he was ...'

The marshal said to Lorenzini, 'You see ...'

'See ...?'

'Money ... I have to go.'

The manager got to his feet, looking a bit flustered. 'Marshal, warrant or no warrant, I hope you'll make it clear to the Peruzzis that I wasn't the one to suggest to you anything regarding tax evasion. I'm sure you appreciate . . .'

'Of course. Don't worry. If that's all it is, it doesn't interest me. I'm interested in a murder and a suicide, and a very distressed mother.'

'I understand. We never discussed death duties.'

'I'm sure you were very discreet.'

'No, no, Marshal, I'm quite serious, as you were when you told me you weren't looking to cover anything up and I believed you.'

The man's face was slightly pink but his gaze was straight and unwavering as he offered the marshal his hand. 'It crossed my mind, that's all—and I might add that it also crossed my mind that even a bad-tempered shoemaker can have a past, and that he might be being blackmailed.'

This time it was the marshal's turn: 'Peruzzi? Peruzzi?'

Lorenzini was scribbling something which he pressed into the marshal's hand.

He put on his hat and sunglasses, crossed the road and walked up the sloping forecourt towards the Pitti Palace, wondering why he felt so dreadful all of a sudden.

Someone said, 'Afternoon, Marshal. Isn't this terrible? Let's hope it doesn't keep up all summer.'

'Afternoon . . . yes . . .' The heat. The forecourt was exposed to the worst of it. The sun was beating down, burning through his hat and the shoulders of his uniform. He was tired but he would keep going steadily. That was the thing: keep going steadily. His driver was waiting under the archway in deep shade. Good. He got in and stared for a moment at Lorenzini's scribble, his thoughts elsewhere. Then he read it.

Esposito and J girl on our CCTV 12.04 21 May

It felt like a blow to the stomach, yet his reaction was superficial, just something to be dealt with. He called Lorenzini. 'Can you talk?'

'Yes. I'm still at the bank but the manager's left me alone in his office for the moment.'

'Go on, then.'

'I checked through all the reports for May twenty-first. Esposito was out that morning. He and Di Nuccio went to Signora Verdi's house to catch out those confidence tricksters, you remember, the ones saying they were from the gas company?'

'I remember. And then?'

'Di Nuccio was driving. Going back, Esposito said he'd get out in Piazza Pitti, said he had to do something. Di Nuccio dropped him outside the bank.'

'I see.'

'I looked through the CCTV tapes of our entrance to see what time he came in. He and the girl were outside here at four minutes past twelve. They looked as if they were quarrelling. He looked at his watch and came in. She stood there for a bit, took a few steps towards the exit then turned back and took the main path to the right into the gardens.'

'Did Esposito go out again?'

'I ran the tape on but if he did he wasn't in uniform. There was a fair bit of movement there, people coming from the park keeper's office as well as people coming out of our place with it being the same entrance.'

'Even so, the others must know if he ate with them.'

'He didn't, hadn't done for days. He was always shut in his room when he was off duty, you know that. I've got nothing precise until two thirty when he was with the magistrate dealing with that suicide—man with five kids who lost his job and poisoned himself. So: it's not the perfect alibi like you wanted, not an alibi at all, really.'

'No.'

'What do you want me to do next?'

'Nothing.'

They crossed the river and the driver stopped in via de' Servi at the cathedral end.

'Dott. G. Peruzzi, Accountant, 2nd floor' was engraved on a big brass plate inside the marble entrance. The marshal took the lift up and rang the accountant's doorbell. The door clicked open and at the end of a green-carpeted corridor a tall, elegant man with thick black hair and a pale-grey suit appeared in an open doorway. The marshal was a little disconcerted. At such a fancy business address as this he had expected a flurry of secretaries, perhaps even a long wait. Then the man uttered only one loud word: 'Shit!'

Then he went back into his room leaving the door open.

CHAPTER TEN

He didn't hurry along the corridor. On the contrary, he felt he was slowing down. His footsteps made no sound on the thick green carpet. Perhaps it was that, together with the wooziness caused by lack of sleep, which made him feel he was back in his nightmare. Again his chest hurt with a sort of burning anxiety, his mind quite blacked out. The walk along that carpet seemed to be in slow motion, giving him time to pick up thousands of tiny details, signals, absences. No phones rang, nobody hurried past him, carrying papers from one office to another, although there were many closed doors. A trail of cigar smoke. The corridor opened out at the end into an ample, carpeted space. The marshal was aware of a big desk to his left, of a summery perfume and the thin brown shoulders of a young woman whose eyes were following his progress in silence. He didn't turn his head. His gaze had never left the open door straight ahead. He walked through it and stood still.

'Peruzzi, Gherardo.'

'Present.' Imitating a schoolboy answering to the morning register. He was sitting tipped right back in a leather office chair, his long legs stretched out under the big antique desk, a cigar in his mouth.

The marshal was in no hurry, now. He had all the time in the world to look at the man and his room. It was a big room. There was no green carpet here but polished wood and fine Persian rugs. He'd spent enough time in the antique shops of Florence to recognise the value of the few enormous pieces of furniture in the room. The light fixtures were modern, the paintings on the walls old. The marshal saw himself in a massive mirror that could have reflected five of him, framed in carved and gilded wood which in turn reflected the gold flame on his own hat. He took the hat off, breathed out slowly, met the ironic stare of the man in front of him. He had no intention of speaking first. He knew he'd found what he was looking for. It was enough.

'Are you going to arrest me? Or are you going to sit down?'

The marshal looked about him, chose a solid chair and sat down with his hat on his knee.

'How did you find out? I'm just interested. It doesn't much matter.'

'No. It doesn't much matter. Except perhaps to your father.'

'My father's a fool. As you must have noticed—I take it you know him.'

'Yes, I know him.'

'Spent his life in that poky little dump scratching away at his old-fashioned shoes. A modern factory could churn out a thousand pairs while he's fiddling around with one.'

'Yes, I'm sure you're right.'

'So, how did you find out? Had she said something about her talk with the bank manager to her little boyfriend. She said she hadn't, the bitch.'

'She hadn't. You knew about the bank manager's intention to talk to her, I imagine.'

'Of course I knew. I could hardly do anything but agree. He was threatening to foreclose.'

'Why go so far? Why, when you'd got away with all this'—he gazed at the riches all around him—'for so long, so easily.'

The young man shrugged. 'I fancied a BMW. Had a bit of an accident in the Mercedes. And besides, I wanted to buy this place. Paying rent's a mug's game.'

'Like making shoes.'

'Right.'

'Tell me, do you have any actual clients?'

'A couple. Small stuff. Girl out there deals with them. I don't need to pay her much and she doesn't need to work much. Probably spends her time sending e-mail jokes to her friends.'

'I suppose she was the one who really did your father's accounts?'

'That's what I pay her for, isn't it?'

'She never suspected anything?'

'Why should she? None of her business how my father spent his money, was it?'

230

Your father didn't spend his money.'

'More fool him. He wouldn't know how to. He hasn't a clue about the real world—never put his nose out of that hole of a workshop—do you know how often he and my mother went on holiday? Once. Once! They went to Pietrasanta for their honeymoon. Deckchairs and bicycle rides along the seafront. Christ! Is that pathetic or what? After that, they used to shut in August and go round the museums together like a pair of stupid tourists. Or else on a "nice little day trip", as they called it, to San Gimignano and Siena. I used to say to him:

'Why don't you go abroad, get out of your rut?

'Why should we go abroad? We've got the finest art and the finest buildings in the world right here. And we've got the sea and the countryside and the mountains, not to mention good food and wine and great museums. Where could we go that'd be better than here?

'There ought to be a museum to put him in, and all the Florentines like him.'

'You're a Florentine, too.'

He laughed, a very loud laugh. It could be bravado but it really didn't seem to be. His eyes glittered but not with fear. It was as if he had been rehearsing this for years, waiting for the right audience.

'What about your mother? Was she unhappy with the life she had?'

'You're kidding. She was just as bad as him. Worked in a shoe shop all her life and never went anywhere. And living above the shop. Like the Middle Ages—I can tell you, when I was in my last years at school I never brought my friends home. I mean, can you imagine? I had one friend who lived in a massive house in its own grounds up on the via San Leonardo and another who lived in a villa with a swimming pool in Fiesole. And my mother's saying: —Bring your friends home, they'll always be welcome—I ask you!'

'Didn't they wonder why you never invited them?'

'I told them my mother was an invalid. I wasn't far out. She wasn't that old when she died.'

'Not that old, no.' Luckily for her she hadn't lived to see this day. Once, years ago, Totò had screamed at him,

—Why can't we live in a proper house like everybody else? I can't bring my friends home to a stupid barracks! Why can't you get a real job like other people's dads?

Now, he felt sick and his heart beat too loudly as though he were afraid.

'This room must be air-conditioned, I think . . .' He was cold all of a sudden.

'I've just had it installed. It's super efficient state of the art. If it's too cold for you, I can—'

'No, no . . .' Shouldn't the man sitting in front of him be afraid? If he had no feelings at

232

all for his parents, shouldn't he have some for himself? He must know it was all over. He did know

'*Anyway*; now my father's heart's buggered. He's going to die without ever having lived.'

'He's lived as he wanted to, I think.'

'And what about me?' In a flash of rage, he jerked upright and leaned forward, thrusting a big hand towards the marshal's face. 'What about all those years living over the shop? Years of feeling ashamed—and that wasn't the worst of it. Once I'd qualified and he handed over his accounts, I found out he'd been earning a fortune. Can you imagine how I felt? We could have lived in style!'

He kept on saying 'Can you imagine', expecting the marshal's understanding, his sympathy. Yet he had neither sympathy nor imagination to spare for his father.

'I made him buy a decent flat right away, told him it would be an advantage as regards his taxes and since he never bothered to look at the figures . . .'

'Was that when it started? When you got the idea?'

'No, but it was when I stopped being ashamed of him and started feeling furious instead.'

'You inherited his famous temper, then.'

'I had good reason to be furious, didn't I? Anyway, that's not when it started. My mother was still alive then. She got ill not long after they moved to the new flat.'

'She didn't settle there?'

'She liked the flat. It was a good investment and besides, you can imagine, after that poky old place in the city centre . . . She was always showing it off to people, how clean and bright, how little work:

—I hardly know what to do with myself. Of course, there are some very nice shops at the other end of the avenue, very nice. And a bus stop nearby, too. I don't drive. Gherardo's thought of everything.'

His mimicry was cruel.

'And then she gets cancer.'

'So it started after she died?' That was something . . .'

'With that business of the car. He had that pathetic Fiat. Always refused to buy anything foreign. All his life it was always the latest boring, overpriced offering from Agnelli, saying:

—An Italian car's good enough for me. People buy these foreign cars and then they're paying a fortune for spare parts and trailing around looking for somebody who'll repair them.

'I'd been telling him for years those days were gone, that if he wanted some boring little car he might as well get a Japanese one for half the price that's better made, instead of contributing to Agnelli's vices. In the end, I took advantage of that pyromaniac episode.

234

Set the damn thing on fire myself, claimed on the insurance for him and got him something halfway decent. That was the first Mercedes. Of course, he never drove it.'

'But you did.'

'He never went anywhere. Told me to keep it and started using the bus.'

With a snort of disgust he reached for a marble ashtray and parked his cigar. He had those same long, bony features and thatch of hair, though it was black and his father's grey.

'So what happens next? You get out handcuffs?'

'I haven't got any handcuffs.'

'Well, then?'

'I'll make a phone call. All in good time.'

'Will there be journalists, photographers?'

'Is that what you want?'

He shrugged. Even so, his hand went to his hair and he shot an almost imperceptible glance down at his fine clothes.

The marshal pictured him in court, saying to the judge every few minutes, 'Can you imagine?' He couldn't resist adding, 'It's more than likely the newspapers will make a big thing of it. Your father's a very well-known personality—'

'My father . . .? Oh, I suppose you mean in his own Quarter, in this dump of a town where he thinks the world begins and ends, right?'

'In Florence, yes. Also in a number of other European cities and in Japan. He's a very talented man and he has clients all over the world. He's a rich man, too, isn't he? I mean, look around you. His talent paid for all this.'

'And kept me in misery!'

'In misery? You had a long education, no doubt with all the extras, school trips, skiing week every winter and so on.'

An angry snort: 'The school skiing week in Abetone, two hours from home—my friends went skiing in the high season in the Dolomites or the Alps!'

'He sent you to university, didn't he?'

'Because he wanted it! So he could show off to his friends.'

'That's true. He did show off about it to his friends. Even to me. Would you rather he'd taught you to make shoes?'

'Are you kidding? Even so, I might have had ideas of my own about what I wanted to do. I like cars, for instance . . .'

'You mean you like buying them.'

'What would you know? Have you ever driven a decent car?'

'No. And you're right. What would I know? It's not easy knowing what's the best thing for our children. There's nobody to advise us, no way of practising. When we find out—or think we do—where we went wrong, it's too late.'

'I can hear the violins playing.'

'You have no children yourself?'

'Not me. Never married. I'm more interested in having a good time.'

236

'You're going to prison.'

Again he shrugged. 'It was bound to happen some time. What matters is the world's divided into those who get shat on and those who do the shitting. Unlike my fool of a father, I'm in the second category. And that's where I stay. You'll see when this gets to court. I have a very good lawyer.'

'I'm sure you have. With a taste for expensive things like yourself, no doubt. The truth is, you want it to be over, don't you?'

'What's that supposed to mean?'

'You want the handcuffs, you want the journalists. You want the judge. If you'd been a bit careful it need never have come to this. Your father will die soon. No one would ever have known. And after all, you've only been spending what was to be your rightful inheritance. But you wanted this, didn't you? You wanted me here, listening to your self-justifying whinings. It wasn't enough just to do it, you wanted people to know and say you were quite right. That's it, isn't it?'

'Not people! Him! Him! It's him I hate for the miserable upbringing I had. Years and years of being embarrassed and ashamed. All the money in the world now won't buy me what I needed then.'

'Not what you needed, what you wanted.'

'What everybody else had!'

'There's never any point in comparing ourselves with others, though, is there?

237

There'll always be people who are better off and even more who are worse off.'

'I'm not interested in the others, I'm interested in me.'

'And I'm interested in Akiko.'

'In what . . . ?'

'Akiko Kametsu. Once apprenticed to your father, destined to take over the management of his business, now dead.'

'Oh, her . . .'

'Yes, her. You knew about the bank manager's decision to persuade her to bring your father to the bank. At the very least it would have meant the end of your power of attorney. And had you signed the contract for the purchase of this place? Did you follow her and my young NCO—her little boyfriend, as you call him, also now dead—when they came out of the bank that morning?'

'She must have been worse than my father.'

'What does that mean?'

'I mean that he's a leftover from the age of the dinosaurs but she must have gone into it with her eyes open. Leaving Tokyo to come to this dump, sitting in that hole every day fiddling with shoes—not to mention the boyfriend—no offence meant but really, I mean, how much does somebody like you earn?'

'Not very much. I think, if you'll excuse me, I'll make that phone call now.'

*   *   *

'I've never liked him.'

'Hmph.'

'I don't think he's all that good-looking and besides, he looks the same in every film. That's not acting.'

'Hmph.'

'There's a James Bond film on the other side but it started half an hour ago and you know you can never follow the story, even if you see them from the start . . .'

'Hmph.'

'You haven't told me yet whether you like the new lights.'

'Hmph.'

'Oh, dear. I suppose you heard that the earth was invaded by Martians this morning?'

'No, it wasn't. I have to make a phone call— no, carry on watching.' There was only one film he was concentrating on and that was on a CCTV tape. He switched on the light in the entrance hall and, with the voices of the television film in the background, called Lapo's trattoria. Nobody answered. He looked at his watch. At nine-thirty in the evening, Lapo should be open. He let it ring and ring, tried the number again in case he'd dialled incorrectly. Nobody answered. He hung up and then called the patrol that was out.

'Where are you?'

'Ponte Vecchio.'

'Listen, I want you to check something for me, a trattoria that has to be open at this hour but isn't answering . . .' He told them where it was.

'We can be there in half a minute. What do you want us to do?'

'Nothing. Call me back when you've taken a look.'

He stood there by the phone, waiting, watching the flickering light of the television beyond the open drawing-room door. He lifted the receiver before it could complete one ring.

'Marshal? It's closed. Tables stacked outside, shutters down. There's a bit of paper stuck on that says "Closed because of illness". There's another place opposite that's open. Should we make enquiries there?'

'No. I'll look into it tomorrow. Everything quiet?'

'Fine. Mobile station in Piazza Santo Spirito's had a bit of trouble but it's all quiet now. Traffic's bad, though. The sooner they put the summer ban on driving through the centre at night, the better. It's so hot, it feels like July already. We're stuck in a jam now, can you hear?'

Teresa had changed channel. He sat down to stare at James Bond.

'Is everything all right?'

'What . . .? Oh, yes. I wanted to book a table at Lapo's for Giovanni's birthday supper but he's closed.'

'Closed. Why?'

'For illness, apparently. Probably his mother-in-law. She's had one stroke already.'

'Well, there's no rush. What's the matter with you? What are you looking so worried about? I thought things were going well. Obviously that man you arrested killed that poor girl, so Esposito's name will be cleared. That's the main thing. Such a lovely boy. When I think of his poor mother . . .'

'Yes—is Totò all right?'

'Of course he's all right. You saw he ate his ham and melon, didn't you?'

'And that means he's all right. You're sure.'

'Of course I'm sure. I think you should go to bed. You're still not recovered from that trip to Rome.'

—My son works in Arezzo and he falls asleep in the train but the motorway's so dangerous . . .

But the motorways *are* dangerous . . .

—I don't drive. Gherardo thought of everything.

—I like cars.

Surely, the Peruzzis were good parents. They did their best and yet—

—A stupid barracks! Why can't you get a proper job like everybody else's dad?

What happened to Esposito's father? Would they let his mother see his face, his two faces? Surely to God not . . .

So much danger everywhere.

'Salva!'

—All right . . . Are you coming?'

'I won't be a minute. I'll make us some camomile tea. Get into bed and I'll bring it through.'

Later, when the light was out, he said, 'Do you remember Totò screaming at me that time, telling me I should get a real job like other people's dads?'

'No.'

'No? *No?*'

'When was this? Not recently?' She yawned.

'No, no. Years ago. That time when he got in trouble, pinching stuff from a department store with his friends when they were supposed to be at gymnastics.'

'Oh, that. He was probably frightened you were going to arrest him. That was a bad patch he went through. How can you remember a detail like that?'

'How can you forget it? I was very upset.'

'So was he. But, as I remember it, he was upset because you wouldn't let him have a cat.'

'Cat? What cat?'

'That stray. You know, it ended up in Boboli with all the others but you and Totò went looking for it together. I don't think you ever found it.'

'I don't remember anything about a cat. I just remember him flying at me, attacking me.'

Teresa turned to him and settled down with her arm across his chest. 'Thank goodness he has you. He's sensitive and he gets so edgy. Then he crashes against you and you're there, as solid as an oak tree. That always calms him down.'

'But I never know what to say to him.'

'It doesn't matter what you say. Don't say anything. Now go to sleep.'

'I can't help thinking about Esposito and Akiko. I mean, if you think about us, we come from the same town. We didn't just know each other, our families knew each other for two or three generations at least.'

'Times have changed. And don't forget my Aunt Carmela—you remember, my father's younger sister. She died not long after we got married.'

'Yes, but what's she got to do with Esposito?'

'With Akiko, running away from her family. Not that Aunt Carmela ran away but she did hate the whole business of everybody knowing everybody in Noto, commenting, gossiping, criticising. She started going out with boys from Siracusa and eventually married one. It was a big scandal at the time, her behaviour. She had to be up to no good if she didn't want to be seen and so on. And everybody calculating the dates when her first child was born. It followed her all her life, that suspicion. She told me herself that she wasn't up to no good at all. The only reason was that she hated everybody knowing her business and talking it over, thinking they had a right to comment or even interfere. I can understand that.'

'Yes but . . . Akiko died in a foreign country. She's lying in a refrigerated drawer with no face.'

'Have you heard from her parents?'

'The captain's in touch with the consulate. I can understand her running away. Arranged marriages, after all, these days . . . But you need people around who really know you, don't you? Who've known you all your life, know who you are?'

'I hadn't thought. I suppose you're right.'

'Maybe it's just a question of getting the right balance.'

'Or just luck. Let's go to sleep.'

*   *   *

Esposito wrote to his mother before he killed himself. It wasn't a letter of goodbye—or, at least, he pretended it wasn't. He must have been fighting against what he felt was happening to him right until the very last moment when he heaved himself out of his seat in the train with the strange groan that impressed all his fellow passengers in one way or another. When Akiko vanished from his life and, as he thought, stopped answering the telephone, he went to Peruzzi who thought she was in Rome. He went to Rome and found no

244

one. Then her friend came back from Tokyo and unwittingly gave him the false news that, for Esposito, meant the end of everything.

'She must have hated me.' He wrote that to his mother, as he'd said it to Toshimitsu.

But it wasn't true. She hadn't gone through with it and the sad thing was that he died not knowing that.

The marshal read the last part of his letter with some apprehension because it referred to himself.

He's given me leave to come home but I got off the train here. I wish now I'd told him everything. I have told him in my head a hundred times. Only, he has such faith in me—he's even talked about the possibility of my becoming an officer one day. It can happen. I don't want to let him down. He's not going to see me as officer material if he finds out what I'm really like, incapable of dealing with my private life, letting it spill over into my work. At least, as long as I'm busy, it's not too bad but when I'm not working everything's so black I can't breathe. I'm not taking anything. I've got to deal with it. I'm sorry. I'm really sorry. I'm in this little hotel. The room's very small and there's this painting of the bay of Naples. I told her you knew, that you'd look after her. She could stop work right away and move in with you until we're married. How could she have done it without telling me? I wish the marshal were here now. It wouldn't matter whether I told him or not. I wouldn't care what he thought of me, what he said to me if he were just here. Nothing seems real or solid. I can't get a grip on anything and I'm frightened I'm going to let everybody down. I'm sorry.

The marshal looked up from the photocopied sheet, puzzled.

'It stops there,' the captain said. 'As you can see, it was written on hotel stationery. He didn't finish it or sign it but he put it into an envelope and sealed it at some point. It was in his back pocket. Naturally it was sent with the rest of his effects to his mother. I spoke to her myself.'

'How is she?'

'As you'd expect. I got the impression that she'd been afraid all along that it might end like this. She said:

—He was so like his father. I never told him so and he really had no memory of him. My husband, Gennaro, was a lovely man, so handsome, but he took things too much to heart. He had rheumatic fever as a child and his mitral valve started giving him trouble when he was only in his thirties. In the end he was too sick too often to hold down a job. He felt he'd let us down, that I'd be tied to an invalid all my life and I should never have married him. Naturally, nobody would insure his life. I never talked about it to Enzo— should I have done? People get shot every year when the hunting season opens so I thought, if he heard anything, he'd just assume there'd been an accident. I gave Gennaro's revolver to one of his friends to dispose of. It might have been better, after all, if we'd talked about it. And besides, it's as if he knew . . . after all, Enzo wasn't on duty, he wasn't in uniform, so why was he carrying his gun? Children sense the things we don't tell them . . .

'She asked me to thank you particularly.'

'Me?' The marshal was surprised.

'He always told her you were a father to him. I had the impression she felt he was more in need of a father figure than a wife for the time being. Incidentally, the magistrate has released the body. I was able to tell her that, at least I'm sorry I couldn't help you as regards the autopsy, but as I said . . .'

'No, no . . . It didn't matter, as it turned out. Forli was able to help. She can bury her son without the added distress of any suspicion. I hope so, anyway . . . And Akiko?'

'They'll release her body tomorrow and the consulate will take over from there. What about your case? How's it looking?'

'Not good. Peruzzi's not going to testify against his son so we lose our motive, for what

247

motive's worth, and we've no physical evidence and no witnesses.'

'What about the bank manager?'

The marshal shrugged. 'Peruzzi's son had power of attorney. We'd need more than that.'

'I thought he'd confessed to you?'

'He tried to, for what it's worth, given that we were alone and I hadn't warned him of his rights. He seems convinced that I'm bound to agree he did the right thing—but you know who his lawyer is?'

'I know.'

'Well, then. He's already pointed out that nothing that was said before his arrival on the scene has any validity. The first story he came up with was that his client was nowhere near the scene, didn't follow the couple, etc. etc., that I'd invented the whole story. That's when I told him about the CCTV footage. It showed Akiko hesitating and then going into the gardens. Once we knew she'd been followed, we ran the tape on and saw Gherardo Peruzzi hurrying after her. The delay was because he had to buy a ticket. Akiko had come in the gate with Esposito. Once he hears this, the lawyer comes up with a new story, admitting his client's involvement but claiming that after a chat on the ledge of the pool, she had lifted her feet to show him the shoes she'd made and it was when he got hold of one to examine it that she fell back into the water. There's probably something of the truth in that, for what it's worth.'

'And then? He left her to drown?'

'Oh, not at all. The water's very shallow. It never crossed his mind that she'd drown, only that she'd be annoyed with him for causing her a soaking. So he rushed off.'

'Taking with him the shoe that came off in his hand?'

'And the bank receipts and all her documents but everything went down that drain except for the shoe which stuck. Anyway, the lawyer's requested the CCTV film and when he sees it's not a good enough full-face picture of his client, he's likely go back to story number one. In any case, whatever damn-fool story he brings to court in the end, he'll throw up enough dust and confusion to muddle judge and jury, and make a conviction impossible, given that we have no physical evidence. I ought to tell you that the last time I talked to him he was threatening to drag Esposito's name into it. I've no doubt at all that he saw Esposito go back into the station but that's not what he'll say.'

'He could make it look like a cover-up, is that it?'

'Easily.' Their relationship, the baby the quarrel, the talk of an abortion . . . Gherardo Peruzzi barely knew her and, without his father's testimony, he had no motive.'

'I see.' The captain remained silent, thinking. 'He did more or less confess to you, though.'

'Yes. That's what I mean about there being some truth in the second story, about her lifting her feet to show him her shoes. Why wouldn't she trust him? She trusted his father. He said he stood watching her for a bit. She sat down on the edge of the pool and took a package with a sandwich in it from her bag. Only, she didn't eat it. She just sat there with it in her lap looking straight ahead and crying. He went forward, then, and sat down to talk to her. Probably, he pretended to cheer her up. I can well believe he pretended to admire her shoes. He was a Peruzzi. She trusted him.

When we were leaving his office, he took a last look around at his riches and said:

—She was so tiny . . . it was just like flipping a little doll into the water.

'He looked puzzled more than anything. He couldn't understand how such an insignificant episode could make such a change in his life. He'll confess to me again, though.'

'With a lawyer like that? Guarnaccia, you know this man. You know he'll never allow it.'

'Even so. He won't be able to prevent it. His client will insist. He's quite determined to convince me he was in the right. After which the blasted lawyer will get him off with manslaughter anyway. There's nothing to prove premeditation. He had his father's temper. The water was so shallow, the piece of statuary invisible. We can never prove he

250

didn't run off thinking he'd only given her a ducking.'

'And did he?'

'Oh . . . I don't know. To be honest, I doubt if he knows himself. Perhaps, for him, it had no more importance than swatting a fly. Well, it's late. I must be getting back.'

They stood up and walked together to the door. When they got there it was clear to the marshal that the captain had something he wanted to say. They both paused. Without looking at him, the captain said very quietly, 'Somebody else asked me to thank you— though I said you'd be more than pleased if she called you and thanked you herself. I hope I did right.'

'Of course. And she did call me, yesterday evening. It was very kind of the signora even to remember such a small thing.'

'It was important for her.'

'I suppose that's true. I was sorry to hear she's leaving us.'

'Yes. She's completed her researches and has decided she should go home to France to write her book. Her parents are getting frail and she feels she should be near them.'

'Of course.'

The captain's face was strained and very pale. He said goodnight and turned back to his immaculate desk. The marshal closed the oak door and walked the empty corridor to go down to the cloister. The streets outside were

251

darkening. The marshal was anxious to be home.

*   *   *

That first year that Teresa and the boys moved up to Florence, the marshal hadn't been able to resist teasing Giovanni about his combined birthday and name day:

—The mayor has organised a huge firework display and the Palazzo Vecchio—you remember, the one with the tower where the mayor's office is?—well, it's going to be lit with torches like a castle in a fairy tale . . .

The solemn little boy had listened, wide-eyed and silent. He had still been too excited to speak when they went out into the blue night to lean on the warm parapet of the Santa Trinita bridge. Hundreds of families lined the river banks, tiny children perched on dads' shoulders. The street lights went out and the first enormous explosion of pink and gold light burst and sprayed down to meet its own reflection in the black water. Giovanni was too overwhelmed to join in the chorus of ooohs and aaahs. Totò caught on as soon as he saw the crowds but his brother's stunned amazement rendered him quite oblivious to taunts.

When his dad stood him on the bridge, holding tight, he turned his dark head against a glittering green sky to whisper:

—Dad, it's brilliant, isn't it?

Of course, once they started school, he soon found out that San Giovanni was the patron saint of Florence, but the tease became a family tradition:

—Well, the mayor's done you proud again this year . . .

This year, though he was doing his best to seem normal, the marshal had just returned from Esposito's funeral in Naples and, though he'd booked a birthday supper at Lapo's as promised, he almost wished he hadn't because closed shutters and a 'For Sale' sign were an ever present reminder throughout the meal that the predictable second heart attack had spared Peruzzi the pain of his son's trial.

The boys were too excited about the match to notice. Teresa said nothing but squeezed his arm once or twice to bring him back to her.

In an effort to be cheerful, he relayed to her what Lorenzini had told him that morning. He'd gone to last night's dinner and concert at the social club where Nardi was to perform in the presence of both Costanza and Monica. Teresa had been following this story for years.

'And was there a row?'

'There certainly was. Just after he sang "I left my heart in San Francisco" making up half the words, according to Lorenzini, who speaks English. It had been a big meal—'

'Did they have three kinds of pasta like us?' asked Giovanni, looking interested.

'At least. Maybe more. And Florentine beefsteaks.'

'And cake?'

'Probably cake as well. Anyway, after all that, Nardi had sung for almost an hour and he was exhausted. He told Costanza he wanted to go home. She was enjoying herself and wanted to stay. Words were said that would have been better said in private at home and Monica, who was at the next table with her mother—who's almost ninety, incidentally, and eats like a horse—looked up and shouted at Nardi:

—You ought to be ashamed of yourself, speaking to your wife like that and in public, too.

—And you mind your own business! She's my wife and I'll speak to her any way I want!

'He told his wife to suit herself but he was off. He got up and left the table but Costanza didn't budge. After a minute or so, she leaned towards Monica and said:

—He's going nowhere. I've got the car keys and the house keys.

'An hour later the two women were in a huddle and those who were listening in said they came to an ad hoc financial arrangement that suited them both and confidences were being exchanged:

'If you knew what I went through in that first twenty years of marriage, it'd make your hair stand on end. A different one every week. I couldn't hold my head up. And the money it

was costing when we'd two children to bring up.
—It was the same with mine until he had his stroke. After that it was whine whine whine and he wouldn't so much as blow his own nose. Ten years of that I had. It's a good thing we live longer. At least we get a bit of peace and quiet at the last.

'Lorenzini says there's no question of Monica pressing charges for assault.'

'In that case, there wasn't really a row.'

'Yes, there was. I haven't got to that yet. While all this was going on, Nardi was chatting up some woman at another table. Had his arm round her, by all accounts. When they noticed, both Monica and Costanza got up and marched over there. That's when the real row started. Lorenzini had to break it up.'

'You mean they attacked her? Physically attacked her?'

'No, no . . . They attacked him. Got a few good ones in before it was stopped, too. Lorenzini admits he was wary of Monica's nails in particular—and he wasn't in uniform, of course, so they could easily have pretended not to recognise him.'

'Well, all I can say is, there's no understanding what some women see in some men.'

'No . . .' admitted the marshal with a worried frown. 'Perhaps it's just as well. Anyway, Lorenzini says Nardi cleans up well.

He had his teeth in and it seems he has a very good voice for a love song. Seductive, Lorenzini said.'

'Well . . .'

'Birthday cake for Giovanni!' shouted Lapo, carrying it out, held high. He was followed by a very smart young waitress bringing spumante and glasses. The rest of the diners joined in the toast and the singing. Lapo sat with them a while.

The smart young waitress was on loan from the restaurant opposite where the young owner turned out to have a feeling for the Quarter after all.

'It's just for this month. Things get a lot busier in July. But in any case, we can't keep our Sonia at home looking after her grandma for any longer than that. She's been terrific but it's not right to sacrifice her and if the wife stopped at home I'd have to employ a cook. We can't afford that. My mother-in-law could have a third stroke or she could go on for years, bedridden after this second one. There's no way of knowing. What could I do?'

'What will you do?'

'After I've sold up? Well, there'll be a bit of money in the bank. The wife fancies taking over a little stationer's and toy shop not far from here. It'll be a lot less work for her and she's used to a bit of company. I'll probably spend a bit more time in politics. I might be looking for your vote next time round.'

'That won't surprise me at all. Your regulars are going to miss you. Where are they going to eat?'

'Here. That was part of our agreement. My regulars go on eating here at lunchtime at a special all-in price. He turned out to be a decent enough bloke, after all, even though he is Milanese.'

They left for Santa Croce and took their seats in time to watch the first horses in the procession file into the floodlit square. The crowd remained peaceable enough at the passage of judges, halberdiers and guildsmen, but there was tension in the air when the two eliminated teams appeared and a groundswell of aggression rose with the entrance of the finalists. For now it gave vent to nothing worse than carnations raining down like arrows to crisscross the sandy pitch in white and bright dyed blue. The marshal hoped for the best but violence was always to be budgeted for and he thought it likely that he would regret having said yes to this.

But when the canon fired and the first scrum erupted into a fight, Giovanni pulled at his arm. The marshal turned, frowning at the effort to hear him despite the roaring, raging crowd. Giovanni's eyes were popping with the pleasure of pasta and beefsteaks and cake and spumante and football, and fireworks to come.

'Dad, it's brilliant!'

On the other side of Giovanni, Totò, well

fed and happy, was bouncing up and down waving a white flag for Santo Spirito, screaming support. On the marshal's left, Teresa squeezed his arm, whether in enthusiasm or apprehension he didn't know. But the nightmare faded. He started concentrating on the game. You could never tell. Maybe this year the Whites would win.

We hope you have enjoyed this Large Print book. Other Chivers Press or Thorndike Press Large Print books are available at your library or directly from the publishers.

For more information about current and forthcoming titles, please call or write, without obligation, to:

Chivers Large Print
published by BBC Audiobooks Ltd
St James House, The Square
Lower Bristol Road
Bath BA2 3BH
UK
email: bbcaudiobooks@bbc.co.uk
www.bbcaudiobooks.co.uk

OR

Thorndike Press
295 Kennedy Memorial Drive
Waterville
Maine 04901
USA
www.gale.com/thorndike
www.gale.com/wheeler

All our Large Print titles are designed for easy reading, and all our books are made to last.